DEFLECTED HEARTS

WYNCOTE WOLVES #2

CALI MELLE

Copyright © 2022 by Cali Melle

All rights reserved.

No part of this book may be reproduced in any form or by any electronic or mechanical means, including information storage and retrieval systems, without written permission from the author, except for the use of brief quotations in a book review.

This book is a work of fiction and any resemblance to any person, living or dead, or any events or occurrences is purely coincidental. The characters and story lines are created purely by the author's imagination and are used fictitiously.

Cover Designer: Cassie Chapman, Opulent Swag & Designs

Editor: Rumi Khan

Find the love that you deserve and don't settle for anything less, regardless of the circumstances.

PROLOGUE
POPPY

Life has always been a series of ups and downs for me. I came from a broken home, having to divide holidays between two households after my parents divorced when I was ten years old. It was a weird adjustment at the time, especially when I was just entering my teenage years. There are so many things you're experiencing mentally and physically, and then throw in a divorce and it's a perfect triangle of self-despair.

After what I had experienced with my parents, I made a promise to myself that I would never do the same to my children as they did to my sister, Evie and I. I wouldn't have a child, only to have our family and lives fall to shambles.

Evie struggled with it the worst. We were

sixteen months apart, so we were close, but we were polar opposites. I was the quiet one, where she was the one who was the life of the party. She began to act out as we entered high school and wound up in trouble more times than I could count. She blamed my parents for separating and remarrying, instead of trying to work things out and have our family be together.

It was the summer before my senior year of high school when we lost her. Evie was set to leave for college at the end of the summer and there was an annual party thrown at one of the lakes in town. She had just gotten into a fight with our stepmother and father that night and drank more than she should.

It was late at night and Evie had the great idea for everyone to go swimming. A few of the other kids agreed with her, but I begged her not to do it. To just let me take her home, where she was safe, but she refused. We were staying at our dad's house that weekend and she told me she never wanted to go back there again.

That night, she got her wish.

Evie dove into the lake, not realizing that the area was shallow and there were jagged rocks just beneath the surface. Her head collided with one, effectively snapping her neck from the force. I watched her do it and then float to the surface, face-down. Everyone else was too drunk to realize what was going on as I dragged her onto the shore, screaming for help.

Losing her completely turned my world upside down. There were so many what-ifs that hung heavily in the air. My father never quite got over it, especially after the fight they had that night before she passed. He partially blamed me for not preventing it from happening, even though I had tried.

It rocked everyone's lives and, to be honest, I'm not quite sure that any of us truly got over her death. I know I didn't, and the guilt still consumed me from time to time. Maybe my father was right. If I would have tried harder, I could have stopped her from diving in. I live with that every day of my life, because not only did I lose my sister, but I lost my best friend too.

My footsteps are light and dread rolls in the pit of my stomach as I pace up and down the short hallway in my apartment. I glance at my phone, looking at the timer as it begins to count down from ten seconds. The anxiety runs through my system and there's nothing I can do to control it in this moment.

The alarm begins to sound and a ragged breath leaves my lips as I silence it and slide it into the front pocket of my hoodie. I can't believe this is happening right now—that I've gotten myself into a situation like this one, of all things.

My hand finds the doorknob and I slowly turn it as I walk back into the bathroom. I had it closed, as if that would really make a difference. Inhaling deeply, my footsteps are slow as I walk over to the counter. I close my eyes for a moment, wishing for it not to be what I think it's going to be. As I open them, I finally look down at the plastic stick sitting by the sink.

My stomach sinks as my heart crawls into my throat. Two little blue lines stare back at me and it feels as if the rug is being ripped from beneath my feet.

I'm pregnant.

And alone.

The one thing that I never wanted to happen is happening. It would be different if things would have worked out between him and I, but they didn't. He didn't form attachments, and now I'm carrying his baby inside me. A baby that is going to be raised in a broken home, just like I promised myself I would never do.

A sob tears through me, the tears instantly springing to my eyes as I sink onto the bathroom floor. It's been four years since Evie's death and right now, I need her more than anything. She would know exactly what to say or what to do.

I miss my sister... my best friend.

But the only person I have right now is myself.

And August Whitley's baby.

CHAPTER ONE
AUGUST

Four months later

As I step out of the shower, I grab a towel from the rack and wrap it around my waist. Water drips down the sides of my face from my damp hair, but I don't bother drying it as frustration runs through me. Walking over to the counter, I swipe my hand across the moisture that collected on the mirror, creating a thick layer of condensation.

Looking at my reflection, I brush my hand over the healing bruise under my eye. It was one I earned in a fight at a party, because I was stupid and decided to try and pursue a girl I didn't realize had a boyfriend until he was letting me know with his fist in my face. My stupidity got the best of me in that moment and I was jaded.

When it comes down to it in life, hockey will always be the most important thing. I didn't spend my entire life working like I did just to throw it away for some attachment. There was only one girl who made me question that and I went and fucked it up with her. I pushed Poppy away when I couldn't see past my own bullshit.

When we first met, it was something fun, a type of distraction to occupy my free time with. We had both agreed going into it that there would be no strings attached, which then ended up being easier said than done. I never intended to develop feelings for her and as soon as it felt like something more than just messing around, I had no choice but to shut it down.

Poppy and I could never be together, not when we came from two different worlds. And not when mine was already full.

She never expressed how she felt when I put space between us and pushed her away. It's not like she really had the opportunity to, but I kept going back to the bar she worked at anyway like a fucking creep. It wasn't stalking, because I wasn't hiding, but I liked keeping an eye on her, knowing she was okay.

What I didn't expect was for her to move on so quickly and then to vanish. She told me one night that she had a boyfriend, who then proceeded to pick her up. What I didn't find out until later, was that she lied. She didn't move on and it wasn't her boyfriend who picked her up.

It was her cousin, but for some reason she told me it was someone she was in a relationship with, almost as if she was attempting to make it seem like she was doing fine, like she didn't actually need me. And maybe she didn't, but either way, the lie had me questioning everything.

I never got the chance to ask her the questions I had because shortly after that, she quit and essentially vanished. Poppy moved out of her apartment—to where, I still don't know. All of her social media accounts were deleted. And no one seemed to know where she ran off to.

And I so desperately wanted to know what she was running from.

Was it me? And if it was, why run?

Grabbing another towel from the rack, I drape it over my head before viciously drying my hair. It messes it up, leaving the natural waves tousled on the top of my head. I stare at myself in the mirror, my hazel eyes looking back at me through my reflection. Picking up my phone from the counter, I look at the time and groan.

I have half an hour until I'm supposed to pick up Bailey. There was nothing serious between us. Hell, I had just met her a few weeks ago through my sister, Isla. They are both in an art class together and Isla decided it would be in my best interest to try and find someone else to occupy my time with. The idea sounded nice at the time and we started talking after Isla gave me Bailey's number.

We've only met once, more so in passing between classes. I don't know why I agreed to this date, but Isla insisted I do it. To try and make a better effort and do things the right way this time instead of how I went about everything with Poppy... because we all saw where that got me.

And, of course, my best friend, Logan, took Isla's side. I wouldn't have expected anything less from him because since they started dating, he always seems to be team Isla instead of team August. I can't say that I blame him, though. She has more common sense than I do.

I quickly towel off my body and slip into my clothes that I brought into the bathroom with me.

Grabbing my deodorant from the cabinet, I apply that under my arms and spray some cologne on before giving myself a once-over in the mirror. I run my fingers through my hair, working through the knots before leaving it in waves that hang down above my eyebrows.

Bailey picked somewhere that was more low-key, so I didn't need to dress up, but I don't want to show up there looking like a bum. My typical outfit consists of sweatpants and t-shirts and hoodies. It wasn't really a suitable outfit for tonight, so I settled on a pair of dark-washed jeans and a dark gray Henley.

I clean up everything in the bathroom and spray down the shower with the daily spray that we have before slipping out of the room. The air feels cold as I step out into the hallway and walk down to my room and drop my dirty clothes and towels in the hamper by my closet. I grab my coat from where it hangs on the back of my door and head back out of my bedroom.

Isla and Logan are sitting on the couch, watching some movie as they eat Chinese food from boxes with chopsticks. Logan glances over at me, a smirk on his face as he gives me a once-over.

"Damn, Whitley," he whistles, being dramatic as

hell. He's annoying, but I must say that the relationship he's developed with my sister looks good on him. He finally looks happy. And even though I wasn't on board with it at first, I saw how they were together, and put my feelings aside to make sure the two of them were happy. They've grown on me now as a couple.

I just hope my best friend doesn't hurt my little sister, or I'll have to hurt him.

"You look good, August," Isla smiles at me, tilting her head to the side. "I think this might be one of the first times in years that I've seen you dress up, besides wearing a damn suit for some kind of hockey event."

Rolling my eyes at the two of them, I head into the kitchen and grab a bottle of water, swallowing almost half of it in two gulps. "Is it too late to cancel?" I ask both of them as I stroll back into the dining room. "Movies and Chinese food sounds a lot better than small talk at a restaurant."

"Absolutely not," Isla scolds me, sounding like our damn mother. "You can't cancel on her now. You have no idea how excited Bailey is for tonight and even if things don't work out, you can still give it a chance and try to get to know her."

"I can already tell you, there's nothing there besides platonic feelings."

Logan purses his lips, shaking his head as he pops a piece of chicken into his mouth. "Dude… you've made no progress on finding Poppy. Don't you think it's time to let it go? Maybe she doesn't want to be found."

The anxiety has my heart racing, pounding erratically in my chest. My emotions are one thing I've never been good at concealing and keeping in check, except for on the ice. My palms begin to sweat at the mention of Poppy's name alone. Logan's right, I have gotten nowhere in my search for her, but I don't know that I'm ready to give up that easily.

But then again, I did make plans with Bailey to try and get over Poppy. It's probably not the best way to get over someone, especially someone you were never in a relationship with. I was the one who ruined things with Poppy because I didn't want to feel. I didn't want to have that attachment because I've seen what it does to people, I've seen what it can do to their careers.

I need to let her go.

Inhaling deeply, I let out an exaggerated breath as I look between the two of them. "You're right. I owe it to myself and to Bailey to at least try. Maybe there isn't anything there with her now, but I don't really even know her yet."

"Good." Isla smiles at me, nodding as she twirls her chopsticks in her noodles. "There's not enough Chinese food here to share with you anyways."

A laugh falls from Logan's lips and he glances at Isla, his gaze only for her. I would be lying if I said there wasn't a part of me that didn't want what they have. Logan is as focused on hockey as I am, and seeing him be able to make a relationship work at the same time has definitely been an eye-opener.

"Whatever." I drink the rest of my water from the bottle and crush the plastic between my palms before chucking it at the two of them. "I can't make any promises, but I'm going to at least try tonight with her."

Isla smiles at me with understanding and approval in her eyes. "That's all you can do. And if it doesn't feel right, then just be honest with her."

Bailey texted me when I was walking out the door that she would just meet me at the restaurant, which honestly sounded like a better idea to me anyway. It's not that I wouldn't have given her a ride, but by driving separately, it doesn't make it feel as forced that the night has to continue after we're done at the restaurant.

It takes me a little longer to get there, since the place she chose is in the next town over. When I get there, she's already inside, waiting for me at our table. I see her from across the restaurant, her blue eyes scanning the menu as I walk over to her. She lifts her head, her long blonde hair framing the sides of her face and a smile touching her lips as I take a seat across from her.

"Hi, August," she says, her voice soft and gentle. "I was waiting for you to get here before ordering any drinks."

I smile back at her, settling in my seat as I grab the menu in front of me. "You didn't have to wait for me, but that was very kind of you. I'm just going to have water because I have a game tomorrow."

"Of course." She smiles, a pink tint creeping across her cheeks in embarrassment. "I completely forgot you said that you had one tomorrow so I apologize for not thinking about that."

I nod in understanding. I can't expect her to remember my schedule, so I attempt to let it roll off me instead of frustrating me. I can't have any expectations of her when I don't even know her. If there was one thing Poppy always knew, it was how important hockey was and will always be.

I need to stop comparing everything to her when this date is just getting started...

Our server walks over to us, and I lift my head as she stops in front of our table. My eyes widen as the air quickly drains from my lungs and catches in my throat. She stares back at me with a look of shock washing over her face.

She quickly recovers, directing her gaze to Bailey. "Are the two of you ready to order drinks?"

I can't take my eyes away from her, my gaze trailing down her torso. Her black t-shirt hugs her curves, her breasts fuller than I last remembered. And it isn't until my eyes reach her stomach that I feel like all of the oxygen vanishes from the room. Beneath the apron tied around her waist is a round bump, her belly sticking out like it's swollen.

Holy fuck...

She's pregnant.

CHAPTER TWO
POPPY

This literally cannot be happening right now.

I want nothing more than the ground to open up and swallow me whole.

August's eyes are glued to my stomach, the color draining from his face as he stares at my protruding belly. I'm only a little over four months, but because of my smaller frame, it's been much harder to conceal and I'm showing more than I'd like to at this point. I didn't think it would be much of an issue, though, until this moment. There was no one that I needed to hide it from because he was the last person that I had expected to see.

But now he's here... on a date with another girl, staring at my pregnant stomach where his baby is growing inside.

"August..." The girl stares at him, her eyebrows drawn together in confusion as her eyes bounce back and forth between the two of us. "Are you okay?"

I watch as his eyes meet hers, his face as white as a ghost. I just need him to give me his drink order so I can go disappear and maybe find someone else to cover my table. There's no way I can work under this tension and the awkwardness that hangs heavily in the air.

August almost entirely ignores her, his mocha-colored eyes meeting mine in a rush. "Give us a moment," he says, his voice low and eerily calm.

"Okay," I say slowly, attempting to keep the panic from my voice as I attempt to take a step back. As I move to turn away from them, his arm darts out, his hand wrapping around my wrist. I look back at him over my shoulder, my eyebrows drawn together in confusion.

"Not you." He glances at the girl across from him. "I'm sorry, Bailey." His voice is heavy with regret. "I'll be right back. I need to talk to Poppy for a minute."

Shit.

My stomach sinks and bile instantly rises up my throat, burning my esophagus. It's been a while since I've had any morning sickness, but this is entirely something different. The adrenaline is rocking my system and I'm ready to run again as my flight mechanism begins to kick in.

"Uh, okay," Bailey practically whispers, the hurt and confusion washing over her face. And I've never wanted to disappear as badly as I do at this moment.

August rises to his feet, his six-foot frame towering over mine. His hand doesn't leave my wrist as he walks past me, pulling me along with him. "Where's somewhere we can talk in private?"

My eyes are on the back of his head, the tousled soft hair I loved running my hands through when his face was buried between my legs. A heat creeps up my neck, spreading across my cheeks as I brush the thought away from my mind. "Outside," I answer, my voice sticking in my throat like peanut butter.

I follow August out front, ignoring the glances from my coworkers as we slip out into the darkness of the evening. There's a chance I might get fired after this, but he's not going to let me out of his sight right now before he says whatever it is he needs to get out.

He leads me to the side of the building, instantly

releasing my wrist as he stops. His shoulders heave as he takes a deep breath and slowly turns around to face me. "You're pregnant?"

My lips part and I stare back at him in utter shock. All I can do is nod because I don't fully trust my voice with the way he's looking at me right now. I watch his eyes transform, a wave of pain washing over his brown irises.

"Is this why you lied?" There's nothing harsh in his tone, just curiosity and hurt. "I know that was your cousin and not your boyfriend. Is this why you quit at the bar and moved out of your apartment?"

My eyes widen and I shake my head. "I just found out and we weren't on speaking terms. You made it clear that there wasn't any room for me in your life and that's okay. I don't blame you for that, August. We went into that situation with no strings attached. I didn't want to burden you with any of it and I was tired of working at the bar.

"I moved back home with my parents so I could focus on finishing my degree before the baby comes and not having to work as much. I just work here part-time... and I should probably get back inside."

I make an attempt to walk around him, but he quickly steps to the side, his movements faster than mine as he blocks my way back to the restaurant. I can't fully read the expression on his face as he attempts to process everything I just said, but I'm just being honest with him. I didn't run—instead, I retreated to somewhere safe, somewhere that would give me the chance to get my life in order so I wouldn't have to struggle supporting a child by myself.

August's eyebrows draw together, his eyes burning through mine. "Is it mine?" His voice is hoarse and thick with emotion.

I've been honest with him so far, but am I ready to come clean about this? He deserves to know, but I'm terrified to tell him the truth. The last thing I want to do is cause any turmoil in his life, to cause any complications. That's all a baby will do. It wouldn't take much for both of us to become a burden to August and interfere with his perfectly structured life.

"Poppy!" My manager yells my name as she stomps around the corner to where we're currently standing. "If you want to keep your job, you need to get your ass back inside."

I use her anger as a distraction and quickly duck around August without another word, leaving him in the darkness of the night with his question still hanging heavily in the air. As we head back into the restaurant, I pause at the door, my eyes meeting his as he walks toward us. He left his date inside and now he needs to go back in to her.

I've already got a plan to ask someone else to cover their table, because I can't face him right now. His eyes are narrowed, a shadow passing over his face that sends a shiver straight up my spine.

I may not be able to answer his question and face him right now, but something about the way he's looking at me tells me he's going to give me no choice. He's not going to let me go that easily this time. He isn't going to let this rest until I give him a straight answer, until he knows the truth.

August Whitely is nowhere close to being done with me.

And there's nowhere else for me to run.

CHAPTER THREE
AUGUST

As I walk in the door of the apartment, I notice that it's already dark and quiet inside. My mind is still reeling from the disaster of an evening and I'm even more confused than I was before. There's a part of me that wishes I wouldn't have seen Poppy, that I could have finally let her go... but then my mind travels back to the most important part.

The fact that she's fucking pregnant and I'm almost positive it's mine.

I don't know what Poppy has been doing since we were last together, but she practically confirmed she found out she was pregnant right after we stopped talking and hanging out. We never really discussed it at the time, because we weren't exclusive, but I don't think she was seeing anyone else... I don't really know, though, without her coming clean.

And, obviously, telling the truth doesn't seem to be her strong suit.

After we went out to talk and she abruptly got pulled back into the restaurant for her shift, I collected myself and got my shit together before I went back in to Bailey. She seemed pretty confused and disappointed by the entire situation with Poppy, even though she didn't know everything and didn't have the backstory.

I didn't tell her what had happened in the past, but I told her that Poppy was someone I used to see and seeing her pregnant caught me off guard. When Bailey asked me if it was my baby, I told her the truth—that I don't know, because truthfully, I don't. And just the thought of how Poppy left me hanging with that unanswered question made my blood boil.

It made my anxiety rise higher than it has ever been and I feel like I'm coming apart at the seams. I so badly want to just pick up a bottle and drown my sorrows and pain right now, but I'm trying to be better. I have a game in the morning and getting shitfaced to try and deal with my emotions isn't good for anyone. Especially when I'm trying to get my shit together and stop traveling down the path that I've been heading down.

Bailey didn't seem too comfortable with the entire situation between Poppy and I. I can't say I blame her and until I get the answers I need, I'm not in the right headspace to get involved with someone else. When I explained that to Bailey, she was more understanding than I anticipated her being.

Instead of continuing the night like it was a date, we simply took the time to get to know each other on a platonic level. She didn't disagree when I asked her if we could go somewhere else because I no longer felt comfortable at the restaurant. Poppy pawned our table off to another server and while I was grateful to not have to face her anymore, I couldn't stand being in her presence. She was still floating around the restaurant, avoiding eye contact with me the entire time.

I needed to get her away from there and have a real conversation with her, but I needed to approach this differently than I had in the past with her. I already scared her off once, and I wasn't about to do that again. Seeing me was just as much of a shock to her as it was to me, so even though space isn't my thing, that's what she needs right now... but this isn't over. Not until I get the answers she owes me.

And depending on what they are determines what the hell happens from here.

Bailey and I ended up at a diner instead, leaving a tip on the table before we went there, even though we never got around to ordering any food. It was the least we could do for taking up a table. We went to the diner, got some breakfast for dinner, and called it a night as just friends. It was the right thing to do and I was glad that she wasn't mad, and instead agreeable.

I walk through the silent apartment, fighting the urge to begin pacing as I head into my bedroom. Stripping down to my boxers, I climb under the covers and pull them up to my chin as I flop onto my back and stare at the ceiling. I know sleep won't be finding me tonight, but tossing and turning for hours is better than drowning myself in a bottle.

My alarm begins to go off, beeping loudly on my phone, but I'm already awake. Swinging my legs over the bed, my feet hit the hardwood floor as I grab my phone and turn off the dreadful sound. Sleep found me in small increments throughout the night, but every time I started to fall into a deeper state of slumber, my dreams forced me awake.

They were more like nightmares, and that's something I struggled with in my teenage years. No one was really ever able to figure out what the root cause of them were, but it was suspected that it had to do with my anxiety. And given the chain of events last night, it's safe to say my anxiety isn't exactly in check right now.

As I roll my bag out of my room, I see Logan already in the kitchen, making protein smoothies for both of us. He has a pair of sweats and a hoodie on, since we usually change at the rink in the locker room. I'm wearing basically the same outfit, with my hood pulled over my head in an attempt to shield myself from life.

"How did last night go?" Logan questions me, his blue eyes searching mine as he hands me my smoothie.

I take a small sip and shrug. "It wasn't what I anticipated, but we both agreed we're better off as friends."

Logan narrows his eyes at me, grabbing his keys from the counter as he heads over to the door where our sticks are propped up. We both grab ours and wheel our bags through the front door. "Did something happen?"

"I don't really want to talk about it right now," I tell him, attempting to keep the irritation from my voice. There's no reason to project it onto him, but right now I don't need him questioning me. Especially at six o'clock in the morning when I barely got any rest.

Logan doesn't question me any more, dropping it as we fall into an awkward silence and load our stuff in his car before taking off to the rink. It's a home game today, so we don't have to travel far, but we still have to be there early enough to warm up.

When we arrive at the arena, Logan still doesn't say anything, silently handing me both of our sticks as he pulls our bags from the trunk. We each take our own, wheeling them into the locker room in silence. The guys are already there, acting like it's not the ass-crack of dawn right now.

I don't really talk to anyone and the air seems to shift in the locker room as Cam attempts to talk to me, but I brush him off, telling everyone that I didn't get much sleep, so they know better than to fuck with me. We all get dressed and head out onto the ice for warm-ups.

Logan skates over to me as we shoot a few practice shots after stretching. "Did you hear the news about King?"

I look over at him, my eyebrows drawn together in confusion. Hayden King was one of our friends from high school, one of the guys we played hockey with our entire lives growing up. When we left for college, Logan, Cam, and I ended up here and Hayden went up to Maine to attend school there. We still keep in touch, but not as much as when we were playing together all the time.

"He's transferring to Wyncote. Some shit must have happened in Maine and he needed to get out." Logan shrugs, raising his eyebrows suspiciously. "He didn't tell me what happened, but his parents were able to pull some strings and get him on the team with the season already started."

I'm not surprised. Hayden comes from money, and money talks. Plus, with his skill on the ice, our coach would be an idiot not to take him on the team. I'm excited to see one of my oldest friends and play with him again, but I can't get the fucking thought of Poppy out of my head.

"Yo." Logan's voice is loud as he hits me in the

thigh with his stick. "Did you hear a word I said? What the fuck's going on with you?"

My eyes meet his as he glares at me through the cage of his helmet. "Is Isla coming to the game?"

Logan's eyebrows draw together. "Yeah, she was driving separately because she didn't feel like coming early while we warmed up."

"Maybe we can go get lunch then? I need to talk to you guys after the game..."

Logan tilts his head to the side, eyeing me suspiciously. Warm-ups are over and we're being ordered off the ice so the Zamboni can come out and clean the ice before the game. Logan skates beside me, his eyes still on the side of my face. "About what? What's going on, August?"

I swallow hard over the lump in my throat. "When I was out with Bailey last night, I saw Poppy." I pause, glancing at Logan as he stops short, before continuing to skate beside me. "She moved back with her parents. She's been here the entire time—so fucking close in North Point, I just had no idea."

"I'm glad you found her, but what do you expect to happen now?"

"I don't know, man," I mutter as we walk down

the tunnel into the locker room. "But she's pregnant."

Logan's eyes widen, his lips parting slightly. "Oh fuck," he breathes, his voice barely audible. "This changes everything."

No truer words have ever been spoken...

CHAPTER FOUR
POPPY

Seeing August wasn't what I expected to happen Friday night. After running into him, I can't help but question my decision to disappear from his life. I still stand by it because he has enough stuff going on in his life and the last thing I want to do is disrupt it... but the look on his face when he saw my stomach, I can't erase it from my memory.

It's Monday morning and my weekend shifts are over, so now it's time to switch back into school mode so I can focus on my classes this week. I'm literally so close to finishing and I'll be graduating a year early with the way I've loaded my schedule. It was always my plan, but since getting pregnant, I need to make sure I'm done before the baby comes.

After losing my sister, I had this drive inside of me to help others. I toyed around with the idea of being a psychologist and working in the mental health field for the longest time after seeing Evie's struggles. I'll be finishing my bachelor's degree this spring and will still need to continue my masters to make that happen, so for now, I plan on going into social work.

After the baby comes, I can always take online classes in the evening to work toward my end goal. It won't be easy, but I just want to do something good in the world. I want to make a difference in someone's life. I know social work isn't where I want to stop, but it's a starting point.

And we need as many of those as we can get in life.

As I get dressed for class, my mom pops her head into the bathroom door. Her bright blue eyes meet mine. "How are you feeling this morning? Do you have classes all day?"

I nod, curling my wrist as I add the wing to my eyeliner. "I should be home around dinnertime. And I feel like I do every morning... freaking tired."

My mother laughs lightly, flashing her bright white teeth at me. She's been nothing but supportive since I found out I was pregnant, even though she has no idea who the father is. Unlike my father, who I lost touch with after Evie's death, she's been involved in my life every step of the way. She picked up the pieces whenever they fell and was always a shining light in the darkness of life.

She remarried after the divorce and she's been with Benjamin since. Growing up, we came from a middle-class family, but when she married him, our lives changed for the better. He is a lawyer, who makes a cushy income. My mother, though, she still refuses to be dependent on a man after things went south with my father.

Even to this day, although she doesn't have to get a job, she still wakes up every morning and goes and works her nine-to-five job as a librarian. I honestly think she just needs the escape, that she would go crazy if she sat at home by herself every day doing the same monotonous bullshit. Losing Evie was hard on her too, but she accepted it as the accident it was.

There was nothing any of us could do to change what happened. Nothing was going to bring her back, and my mother clung to me even harder, since I was her only surviving child. She didn't spoil me in that sense, but she always made sure I was okay and had everything I needed. We were close before Evie passed away, but her passing added a new level of closeness to our relationship. That was the only positive thing that came from her death.

My father, however... he moved on with a brand-new family, essentially replacing us. Even though he was remarried before Evie died, it's like I was a painful reminder and just my existence made him cringe. It was hard for me to accept at first, but after many therapy sessions and a lot of internal work, I accepted it for what it was. That was just one of his flaws and I couldn't fault him for that. Instead, I made the conscious decision for my own mental health that it was better to sever ties with him. And I couldn't have been happier with that decision.

Especially now that I'm pregnant. He would never accept that, and not having him in my life only made it easier.

"Did you want to go get dinner with me after you're done with your classes?" my mother asks after a moment. "Benjamin has meetings all evening, so I thought maybe just the two of us could go get something to eat and chat."

"That sounds nice." I smile back at her, pulling my braided hair over my shoulder before shrugging on my sweater. "I'll call you when I'm leaving campus."

"Perfect." She beams, pulling me in for a quick hug. "Love you, Pop. Have a good day at school!"

I cringe at her words, a soft laughter falling from my lips. She says the words so casually, like I'm back in middle school, getting ready to go to school. But no. This is more than that. A lot of kids I have classes with mess around and throw it all away. I can't afford to do that. This is more than just attending a university and going to class. My entire future—*our* entire future—depends on this.

As I head downstairs, I hear my mother shutting the garage door before her car disappears down the street. I grab a bottle of water from the fridge and a granola bar before heading out to my car in the driveway. Thankfully, my mom's house isn't far from campus, but I still like to get there a little early to get some studying in before I have to be at class.

And there's one thing that always brings me comfort when I go to class. It's my space, my domain. August may have shown up where I work, but I don't think he knew that I worked there. He was there on a date, for Christ's sake. Thankfully, we don't attend the same university, so he has no reason to be on campus. I don't have to worry about running into him again—reliving that pain.

It shouldn't have hurt me, but it fucking did.

Seeing him with someone else had my stomach in knots and I hated the way it made me feel. I wasn't good enough for him to make more time for, but he could date someone else?

It doesn't matter anymore. I can't focus on that and let August Whitley fuck with my head again. We went our separate ways for a reason and what he does now is out of my control. I can't let it bring me down.

As I drive to campus, his face lingers in my mind. The way he looked when he realized I was pregnant and the possibility of it being his... Hell, his unanswered question had nestled itself inside my mind, worming its way into the darkest crevices of my mind. August Whitley wasn't done with me until he got his answer.

I just need to figure out how to tell him the truth.

I get through my first few classes without any issues. Since I'm only about four and a half months pregnant, the baby isn't too big yet, so I'm not completely uncomfortable or having to run to the bathroom every five minutes. It was terrible at first, with the morning sickness. I almost thought I wouldn't survive it, but I did. Now, I just feel like I'm tired all the time.

And thankfully, I have an hour and a half until my next class. Just enough time to get something to eat and try to take a quick nap in my car. I should really use the time to study for the material we just went over in my morning classes, but I can't stop yawning and I have to give my body the rest it needs. I am growing a damn human inside my stomach right now, after all.

I stop by the café and grab a sandwich and a drink before heading outside. It's nicer out today, even though the air is cold. The bright sun hanging in the sky above is a nice contrast and the warmth it lends soaks through my winter coat, cocooning me in the heat. I find an empty picnic table and sit down to eat my lunch alone.

Unwrapping my sandwich, I take a bite as I glance around the courtyard. Other students sit with some of their friends, all conversing over their meals. I've made a few friends, but none I really cared to reach out to, to spend time like this with. It was weird but I preferred the silence and my own company over having others around sometimes. Especially on a day like this, where my brain is struggling to keep up and I really just want to go to sleep.

"Poppy..." I hear his voice and my body stills, my sandwich falling from my hands onto the wrapper in front of me on the table. I don't bother turning around, but my senses are on high alert. August doesn't go to school here, this is my safe place and he's somewhere he doesn't belong right now.

I watch him from the corner of my eye as he switches from my peripheral vision to directly in front of me and he stands by the picnic table with his hands tucked in the front pockets of his black joggers. My throat feels dry, my heart pounding erratically as it threatens to burst through my ribs and flop onto the table in front of me.

"Is anyone sitting here?" he asks, feigning innocence with a shy tone. His hazel eyes search mine and he shifts his weight nervously on his feet. The sun shines down on his dark hair, highlighting strands as it gives dimension to the soft waves.

Not trusting my voice, I shake my head as I take a large gulp of my drink, my hand shaking as I set it back down. August swings his legs over the bench and sits down in front of me as he folds his hands on the table. Leaning forward, he softens his gaze on mine.

"You're not an easy person to find, Poppy Williams." August tilts his head to the side, a smirk playing on his full lips. "Do you know how hard it was for me to find you? After months of trying to figure out where the hell you went, when you were literally less than thirty minutes away."

"Why are you here, August?" I question him, not taking the bait as I pick my sandwich back up and take a bite of it. It's my feeble attempt to seem unaffected by his presence, by his surprise visit, when in reality my appetite is completely gone and I just want to run back home and curl up under the covers in my childhood bed. "You don't go to school here."

"Oh, I know." He grins, a shadow passing over his expression. "But you do. And you're the exact reason why I'm here."

I sigh, chewing my food before washing it down with another sip of my drink. Setting my sandwich back down, I give him an unamused stare. "What do you want, August?"

"The answer to my question."

He's so simple, so matter-of-fact. It's as if he thinks that I'm going to just spill my secrets that easily, because he asked that of me. I swallow hard over the lump forming in my throat and toy with the thought. I could lie to him—it would be the easiest way to get him out of my face right now. He doesn't deserve that, though. Just because we couldn't make things work between us doesn't mean I can't be honest with him.

After all, this isn't just my secret to keep.

"Ask me again," I challenge him, tilting my head to the side as I fold my hands in front of myself like he did with his.

August's throat bobs as he swallows roughly. He narrows his eyes on mine, chewing on the inside of his cheek as an uncomfortable silence envelops us. He doesn't speak a single word, instead he stares directly through me, as if he already knows the answer without asking the question.

"Is it mine?"

My heart stops in my chest before crawling into my throat. Our surroundings simply fade away and it's just the two of us, suspended in time, hanging by a thread. How easily that thread can be frayed…

"It's yours."

CHAPTER FIVE
AUGUST

The air leaves my lungs in a rush and my head swims from the lack of oxygen. I stare back at Poppy, her blue eyes searching mine desperately as her confession hangs heavily in the air. I had my suspicions, but hearing the confirmation has my entire world spinning around me.

"I'm sorry, August," Poppy whispers, her voice sounding like she's miles and miles away. Tilting my head to the side, a wave of confusion passes over me. It's like she's apologizing because she doesn't know what else to say. "I didn't mean for this to happen."

No. She's not apologizing because she doesn't know what else to say... she's apologizing because she truly feels like she's at fault for this. That she's the one who did this to me. But she's got it all wrong.

"It's my fault," I croak out the words, running a hand through my tousled hair. "I should have been more careful, but figured we were fine since you were on the pill, and I got caught up in the fucking moment." I pause for a moment, my eyes falling to her half-eaten sandwich on the table as my hands curl into fists. "Fuck."

"Look," Poppy starts quietly, a sigh slipping from her lips. "It's neither of our faults. It was an accident and accidents happen. I don't want nor expect anything from you, okay? You asked, so I couldn't hold the truth from you."

My eyebrows draw together and I cut my eyes at her as I lift them from the table. Frustration builds inside, bordering on the edge of anger as I mull over her words. "And what if I wouldn't have asked?" I question her, my voice low and harsh as I stare into the oceanic depths of her eyes. "You were never going to tell me, were you?"

Poppy is silent for a moment, her eyes widening as she swallows hard. "I hadn't made that decision yet."

"And when the fuck were you going to, Poppy?" I

can't control the anger that seeps from my words. "In a few more months? When the baby's born? Or maybe after their fifth birthday?" I pause for a moment, the anger rolling through my body as I clench my fists harder. "What. The. Fuck, Poppy."

Her face falls for a moment, but she quickly recovers, pushing her shoulders back as she lifts her chin in defiance. I watch as the ice glazes over her eyes and her guard is firmly in place, completely impenetrable from my anger. "I was going to tell you when I felt ready to, whenever that may have been. You have your entire life planned out, and you made it clear what your priorities in life are. The last thing I wanted to do was derail your plans with a baby."

My jaw clenches and I blink at her. "Poppy. You're pregnant with my fucking baby. You don't think that's something I would want to know?"

She simply shrugs, picking up her drink as she sucks some of the liquid through the straw. "I don't know." She pauses for a moment, a frown forming on her face. "Like I said, August, you have your entire life planned out. Hockey will always come first for you. Why would I want to impose and potentially mess that up for you?"

I stare back at her, my voice refusing to produce any words as my mouth hangs open slightly. She's pregnant, yet trying to justify not telling me because she doesn't want to mess things up in my life. I don't even know what to think or how to even process her way of thinking. It's not logical in any sense. Of course, hockey is my life, but she's carrying my child now.

"This changes fucking everything," I argue, my voice low and calm. I don't know whether to be more pissed off at her or hurt that she would keep something like this from me. And my mind won't cooperate. I can't convince it to try and see things from her point of view.

"And that's exactly what I don't want," she retorts, shaking her head at me as she checks the time on her phone. "It doesn't have to change anything. I've been fine without you and will continue to be fine. If you want to be a part of the baby's life, I respect that decision. But don't give up everything you've worked for in life because of this."

"Poppy... do you hear your-fucking-self right now?" I can't control the anger in my voice, the hurt that snakes its way around my throat, tightening itself like a vise grip. "You respect my decision if I want to be a part of its life? Do you really think that low of me? That I'm that much of a piece of shit I wouldn't be involved in this?"

Swinging my legs over the side of the bench, I abruptly stand to my feet and run my hands through my hair. I stare down at Poppy as she tips her head back, her eyes finding mine with an icy glaze. A wave of pain passes through her crystal-clear irises and she winces, almost as if my words were a blow.

If anyone is feeling the fucking shrapnel from this, it's me. Deep in my gut, she hits me where it hurts and I don't know how to process this.

"I have to go." My voice is hoarse and rough as I shake my head at her. "This isn't me walking away from you or our child, even though that's exactly what you'd expect from me. I just need to process this and with how abrasive you're being, I need some space."

"That's fine," she says quietly, her voice small, but she straightens her spine, attempting to appear unaffected. "Take all the time you need. We're not going anywhere."

My throat constricts as my heart pounds erratically in my chest, my pulse bouncing out of the side of my neck with such force. "I need your new number. I'll call you later, we can talk about this over dinner."

"I already have plans this evening."

My face contorts and I narrow my eyes at her. "With who?"

My stomach churns at the thought of her carrying my child and going out with someone else. If I find out who it is, they'll have hell to pay.

"That's none of your concern," Poppy responds in a cold tone. A moment passes before her face softens. I watch her tear a piece of paper from a notebook inside her bag and she scribbles something on it with a pen before handing it to me. "I'm going to dinner with my mother tonight."

Her words bring my anger down slightly, but I'm still a mess, my head not knowing what is up or down right now. Relief floods me knowing that I was overthinking and expecting the worst, thinking that she was going out with another guy. This is what Poppy does to me. She clouds my vision and sends me through a whirlwind.

"I'll call you this evening, after I get home from practice," I tell her, waiting for her confirmation. She bites down on her bottom lip, her teeth carving small half-crescent shapes into her plump flesh, and I resist the urge to run my teeth over the marks marring her skin. "Thank you for being honest with me, Poppy."

She swallows hard, her nostrils flaring slightly

as she releases her lips. They part slightly, her chest falling as a ragged breath escapes her, and she nods. I wait for a moment, in case she wants to get another word in, but she doesn't.

I know I shouldn't walk away from her right now, but I need space, and time to process. It fucks with my brain, thinking about how she has known for a few months and didn't want to tell me because she didn't want to disrupt my life...

Doesn't she already know?

She disrupted my life the moment she walked into it...

CHAPTER SIX
POPPY

"Is there something wrong with your food?" my mother asks, breaking through the silence as I push the roasted vegetables around on my plate. "We can send it back if you don't like it. Or are you not feeling well?"

I lift my eyes from the square plate and meet her watchful gaze. "The food is fine, I'm fine. I'm just not that hungry."

"Well, you need to eat, Poppy," my mother scolds me, lifting her glass of wine to her lips as she takes a small sip. "It's not just about you anymore. There's someone else counting on you now too, so staying healthy is the most important thing you can do right now."

Sighing, I continue to push the food around on

my plate, not able to bring it to my lips as my stomach churns. After August left, I hid myself away in my car and had a breakdown. I went there with the intention of taking a nap, but I couldn't get the look on his face out of my head. I couldn't erase the words he spoke that plagues my mind.

"Do you really think that low of me? That I'm that much of a piece of shit I wouldn't be involved in this?"

Of course I don't think any of that of him. I know how driven August is, I know how hard he has worked to get where he is in life, and he's nowhere close to being done. He's shooting for the stars, but he isn't there yet.

Maybe he was right. Maybe I was the one who was wrong and I should have told him as soon as I found out.

"Poppy." My mom's soft voice breaks through my thoughts and she reaches across the table as she places her hand over mine. "What's going on, honey? Something's wrong."

Inhaling deeply, I release my breath in an exaggerated sigh. "I ran into the guy I was seeing before." I pause, swallowing hard as I force the words out. "The father of the baby... I told him."

My mother's eyes widen and she squeezes my hand. "Okay. How did it go?"

"I don't know," I admit, shrugging as the corners of my eyes burn from the tears that threaten to spill. My chin bobs and I bite down on my bottom lip for a moment, forcing the emotions back down. "I didn't think he would want to be involved, but I think I was wrong. He was pretty upset I didn't tell him sooner."

I watch her face transform into something that resembles sympathy but mixed with happiness. "I'm glad you told him," she admits, offering me a small smile. "I know it's something you had to decide to do yourself, but that baby deserves to have both parents involved, if they want to be."

I nod, the tears burning my eyes again and the emotion bubbling up my throat. Swallowing back a sob, I wipe viciously at my cheeks as the tears spill over, falling down the sides of my face. "I know, Mom. I just didn't think he would want this."

"It doesn't matter what you think or thought, Poppy. What matters is that you know now." She pauses for a moment, squeezing my hand again as I continue to swipe at the tears that keep falling. "Don't forget that it's okay to let yourself feel. I know you tend to shield your emotions from people, especially after we lost Evie. It's okay to let people in sometimes. It's okay to let them see the real you—the good, the bad, and the ugly."

Her words hit me straight in my core and it feels as though my heart is coming apart at the seams. I stare back into her ocean eyes that mirror my own and nod, smiling at her through my tears. "Thank you, Mom... for everything."

Words could never fully do it justice, the amount of appreciation I have for this woman is unworldly. When it comes down to it, she will always have my back, regardless of what happens. And I know that once I have this baby, I will strive to be just like her.

I just hope August will do the same for our child.

After we get back to the house, my mom heads to bed to do some reading before going to sleep. Benjamin was already here when we got home, waiting for her as he was watching some documentary in the living room. He greeted her with a warm smile and a kiss, like he always does before they go upstairs.

Benjamin is a man who is dedicated to his career. He always has been, since before my mother even met him. But he knew that there were sacrifices that needed to be made, and he made sure that when he married my mother he divorced his career. He is still the best defense attorney in the area, but he always puts his family first.

Even my sister and I. He took Evie's death as hard as the rest of us because when he married my mother, he took a vow to her that he would look after us as if we were his own. And he never fell short of that promise. When my real father stepped down, Benjamin stepped up and he has always been there, supporting me from my mother's shadow. Even sometimes outshining her when he wanted to make sure I knew he was really there for me.

I check my phone, noting that it's already 8:30 in the evening and I still haven't gotten a call from August. A sigh slips from my lips as I grab my slippers and robe and take them into my bathroom. I shut the door behind me and turn on the faucet to the tub after plugging the drain. I don't know August's schedule or when he's got practice, but the fact that he hasn't called doesn't leave me feeling very hopeful.

With it being this late in the evening, I don't imagine that he's still at practice, but I have to give him the benefit of the doubt. He said he would call and I have no reason not to believe him. Instead, I set my phone down on the counter and slip out of my clothes, throwing them into the hamper before grabbing a bath bomb.

I drop it into the water, watching it as it begins to fizz, changing the color of the water to an eggplant purple. The smell of lavender touches my senses, coming from the tub as it continues to fill. I wait until it's deep enough before stepping into the heat. It wraps itself around my legs and my body as I slowly lower myself into the steaming hot water.

If there's one thing that can help calm me down after a rough day, it's a hot bath and the silence. I revel in the silence, where I can be alone with my thoughts, even if they're not always positive. It's the only time I can fully hear Evie's voice clearly anymore. After four years, it's almost like my mind is beginning to forget her, and I can't let that happen.

When everything's quiet, I can hear the lilt of her laughter floating in the air. When I close my eyes, I can see her sparkling blue eyes and the bright smile that was on her face on a good day. I refuse to let myself float to the bad days, to the rough times with Evie. If I want to keep her memory alive, I'll only remember the good. Her death can take the bad and the ugly, because that's not who my sister really was.

Closing my eyes, I slip under the water for a moment, my long hair floating around the top of my head as I allow myself to float in the massive tub. My stomach is the only thing that refuses to go under the water, keeping me afloat like a buoy. Something begins to buzz and I open my eyes, the sounds around me still muffled from the water surrounding my head.

The buzzing doesn't stop, falling into a rhythm. I quickly lift my head from the water, the cool air from the room instantly sending a chill down my spine. A light shines up at the ceiling and I realize that it's my phone ringing. Reaching out of the tub, I dry my hands and grab it from the counter.

I see August's name on the screen and take a deep breath in an effort to calm my heart as it hammers violently in my chest. My efforts are dismal and I reluctantly slide my finger across, accepting his call. Even though I had changed my number, I never got rid of his.

"Hello?" I answer softly, my hand shaking as I hold the phone to my ear.

He's silent for a moment and I hear him release the breath he was holding. "Poppy."

"August." My voice is barely audible, my heart constricting at the way my name sounds rolling off his tongue. "I owe you an apology." I pause for a moment, swallowing back the emotion as my mother's reminder floats into my head. "I'm sorry for not telling you sooner. I was honestly afraid and I didn't want you to feel trapped in any way. I didn't want you to feel pressured to be involved if a baby isn't something you don't want, but it wasn't fair of me to not say anything to you. I should have told you the moment I found out instead of running and hiding like a coward."

"Poppy," he interjects, the sound of my name snaking itself around my eardrum. "Stop. I get it all and you don't have to apologize. I can't blame you for it and it doesn't even matter at this point. All that matters is I know the truth now." He pauses for a moment, his breathing shallow through the speaker. "I'm sorry for the way I reacted. I was out of line and needed to clear my head and process everything."

My heart crawls into my throat at the sound of his apology. "It's okay," I assure him, my voice soft and quiet. "I understand why you would have been upset with me and be mad at the situation. All we can do is move forward."

"I would like that," he admits, the relief evident in his voice. "I want to be involved, Poppy. That baby is mine, too, and just as much my responsibility. Let me be a part of its life. Let me be the father it deserves."

My throat constricts and I swallow back a sob as tears spring to my eyes. These damn pregnancy hormones are making me overly emotional. "I want you to be involved, if you're sure you want to be. I don't want you to feel pressured and I don't want this to be a burden on you at all."

"Poppy, stop," he commands, his voice stern but still warm. "This isn't a fucking burden, okay? You gave me the opportunity to make a choice, but it was never really a choice. The baby is ours, I'm not going anywhere."

I can't stop the tears as they begin to fall from my eyes, streaming down the sides of my face. I'm elated as relief floods my body. The thought of doing this alone was mentally taxing. Keeping the secret from him caused me so much stress. But now, he knows. And he wants to be a part of this.

"I have one condition," I tell him, my voice shaking as I struggle to get the words out.

"Okay..."

"That is all this will ever be. We agreed on no strings attached before, so it has to stay that way." I pause for a moment, swallowing roughly over the lump in my throat. "We can be friends and co-parent, but nothing more."

August is silent for a moment and if I didn't hear his breathing, I would have thought he hung up on me. "You want to be friends with me, Poppy Williams?"

"Yes."

I swear I can almost see the stupid smirk on his face as he chuckles lightly.

"Then I'll be the best friend you've ever had."

CHAPTER SEVEN
AUGUST

Stepping out onto the ice, my skates slide across effortlessly as I adjust my helmet on my head and slip on my gloves. I move over to Logan and Cam as they stretch their legs, getting ready to warm up for practice. We usually do a few different drills, working on skills we need to improve. Every now and then we might engage in a small game, just to practice different plays.

It's been a little more than a week since Poppy and I agreed on being friends, and I'm not sure whether it was a good idea or a bad one. I can't seem to get her out of my head, but it has to be because she's pregnant. Every worry that enters my head has to do with her and making sure her and the baby are safe. I know I'm being irrational, but I hate being away from her when I don't know what's going on.

"So, how's it going, Daddy August?" Cam chuckles as he slides past me, grabbing a puck with the end of his stick. He skates a circle around me, stickhandling the puck absentmindedly.

Logan knew that Poppy was pregnant and after she confessed that it was mine, I had to tell him. He and Isla were more than supportive, and I shouldn't have expected any less. Regardless of what happens in life, the two of them are always by my side. I ended up telling some of the guys on the team, which then spread like wildfire, and now they all know.

"Fuck off, Cam," I roll my eyes, slapping the puck away from him when he isn't paying attention. "You literally saw me earlier today, so don't act like you don't know how it's going."

I've been more irritable lately and projecting it when I should just be swallowing it down. I talk to Poppy every day, but sometimes it doesn't feel like it's enough.

"Did you see King in the locker room?" Logan questions me as he comes between Cam and I. There was nothing hostile between us, but Cam talks a lot of shit and Logan knows that I've been a little unpredictable lately. The last thing I need is Cam to piss me off and me to put my fist through his face. Fighting isn't exactly my thing and fighting our teammates is kind of frowned upon.

I tilt my head to the side, my eyebrows drawn together. "I thought he wasn't coming until later this week?"

Logan shakes his head, stretching out his hamstrings as he spreads his skates apart. "He called me this morning and said some shit changed and he was going to be at practice tonight."

I shake my head, letting him know that I didn't see Hayden in the locker room. "Maybe he's running late or had a change of plans again?"

"Yo!" Hayden's voice calls out as he runs onto the ice, power skating toward us as his skates glide across the clear surface. We both look over at him, a smile forming on both of our lips. It's been a while since either of us have seen Hayden King and he was one of our best friends in high school. "Whitley! Knight!"

He wraps his arms around our shoulders, pulling both of us in as our helmets bump against his. "Shit, I've missed you fuckers," Hayden grins as he moves away from us. "You guys wanna introduce me to the team?"

"Fuck yeah." Logan nods, waving his hands to call everyone in. He introduces everyone to King and they all seem to take to his charming personality. If there's one thing King has always been good at, it is talking to people. He might be full of shit, but he knows how to make his words work for him.

Our coach shows up, calling all of us over after everyone gets their introductions to Hayden King. I hang back, watching as he skates over to our coach and they talk in hushed voices. From what I was told, they had met prior to this, especially since it was the middle of the season. Our head coach would be a fool to add someone to the roster that he didn't know the skill of.

We all break apart into groups after Coach talks to us and we begin working on the different drills. It's tiring and by the time we are done, I'm ready to go home and crawl into bed. We all exit the arena and walk down the alleyway back into the locker room. I drop down onto one of the benches, untying my skates as Cam sits down next to me.

"Some of us are going to go get some food after this," he informs me as he pulls his skates off. "I think Logan said Isla is going to meet us. Did you want to come? I know you've had a lot on your mind lately."

Hayden strolls over, finding his spot on the bench across from me. His deep green eyes meet mine. "What's going on, Whitley?"

"Our boy's going to be a daddy," Asher, our goaltender, says as he walks behind me and taps me on the shoulder like he's actually proud of me. I feel uncomfortable, the way everyone just talks about it like there's nothing wrong with it. Like a baby isn't going to change anything.

"No shit," Hayden muses, his lips curling upward. "Damn, Whitley. I'm surprised that you of all people would be having a baby before you make it to the league."

Logan chokes out a laugh, ducking his head as he slides open the zipper on his bag and shoves some of his gear inside it. "August didn't really have this planned out."

Rolling my eyes, I pull my socks off and shrug off my jersey. "Accidents happen. Sometimes you have to just roll with whatever life throws at you."

"Right," Hayden laughs, shaking his head. "I don't mean to laugh, bro, but I just find it hard to believe. The universe really said fuck you and decided to turn your shit upside down. How do you plan on balancing all of this? You know it's not going to be easy once you get drafted and have to deal with the demands of a professional team instead of college?"

I stare at Hayden for a moment, my eyes narrowing on his. Leave it to him to be blunt and straightforward. I prefer the Hayden King who spews bullshit and tells you what you want to hear, but that's only what he does with the people he doesn't know or when he's trying to get something he wants. Right now, he's being the honest one with no filter. Who feels comfortable enough around me to say whatever he's thinking.

And fuck him for hitting the nail on the head, because this has been my biggest concern.

"I'll make it work," I mutter out loud as they all resume getting undressed and putting their stuff away. It almost feels as if I'm disconnecting, watching the world turning around me.

I'm not sure who I'm trying to convince more... me or them.

My life is about to change, but every aspect of it doesn't have to. Poppy didn't want to tell me because she didn't want to ruin my life and career before it even began. But I can have it all, if I work hard enough. Plenty of professional players have families, so if they can do it, I know I can too.

I leave the guys as they all climb into their cars to get something to eat, and I slip into mine as I pull my phone from my pocket. Poppy's name is the first that shows up in my messages and even though I don't have any unread ones from her, I still tap on her name to call her as I turn on my car. She answers after the second ring, sounding flustered.

"Hey, August," she breathes, the sound of rustling papers in the background. "How was practice?"

"It was good," I answer, putting the car in reverse as I ease out of my parking spot. "Is everything okay? You sound like you're busy."

Poppy sighs through the phone. "I'm just trying to find these notes that I took so I can study for this damn test tomorrow and I can't find them anywhere."

"What class is it for?" I ask her, absentmindedly pulling out of the parking lot and falling into the light traffic on the main road. "Maybe I can come help you."

"Yeah, right," she chuckles, the lilt of her laughter snaking its way around my heart, securing itself to me as it constricts like a vise grip. "It's for a stupid math class that I put off until this last semester because math and I don't really get along."

I laugh, switching lanes with my car as I move farther away from the campus, heading toward my apartment. "I'm not good at math either, but maybe two heads are better than one. Send me your address and let me come help you."

Poppy falls silent for a few moments and I'm afraid she may have hung up. I press my foot down on the brakes as I reach a red light and my breath catches in my throat as I wait for her to respond.

"Okay," she says quietly, her voice shy and timid. "I'll text you it, but let me know when you're here and I'll let you in. I don't need my mom asking any questions."

A smile curls on my lips and I pull a U-turn in the middle of the road, not sure where exactly I'm heading, but Poppy lives at least twenty minutes away and not in this direction. "Your mom would love me."

"That's what I'm afraid of..."

CHAPTER EIGHT
POPPY

August sends me a text, letting me know that he's here. It only took him about fifteen minutes to get to my house and I still don't feel prepared to see him. I glance at myself in the mirror in the hallway before heading downstairs to let him in. As my feet hit the bottom of the stairs, I look around, straining my ears against the silence in an attempt to make sure that the downstairs is clear.

Before I slipped away to my room for the night, my mom said that she would be in the den watching her shows while Benjamin was doing some work stuff in his office. I don't see either of them and I quietly shuffle my bare feet across the hardwood floor as I head over to the front door.

As I pull open the door, a rush of cold air comes in, but my body feels warm as I see August standing there, leaning against the doorway with his damp hair a tousled mess on top of his head. His soft hazel eyes find mine, a smile creeping onto his lips as his eyes scan my outfit, which happens to be an oversized hoodie and pair of fuzzy pajama pants.

"Hey you," he says quietly, stepping toward me as I pull the door open farther for him to step in. "I like your pants." He chuckles, pointing at the white-colored stars on the dark blue material.

"Shut up," I mutter, grabbing his arm as I pull him deeper into the foyer. I quietly close the door behind him, my hand still around his wrist as I lead him toward the stairway. "I don't want my mom to see you."

"See who?" My mom's voice breaks through the silence as she walks into the foyer from the kitchen. Her eyes find August before meeting my gaze. I widen mine, my heart hammering in my chest as the air leaves my lungs. "Who is this?"

August beams, pulling his arm from my grip as he steps toward my mom, holding his hand out to shake hers. "August Whitley. It's nice to meet you."

"Ah, August," she says, her voice soft, a smile

touching her lips as she glances at me. "I've heard a lot about you."

"Oh, have you?" His voice oozes confidence as he looks at me from the corner of his eye. "I hope good things."

I shift my weight nervously on my feet as my mother assesses August. This cannot be happening right now. I can't believe she just blatantly lied to him, but it almost feels as if it were a jab to me. I've mentioned the bare minimum about him after I told her that he knows about the pregnancy. She tried to be understanding, but I could tell there was a part of her that didn't like the fact that we weren't together.

"I'd like to sit down and have a conversation with you sometime," she tells him, her voice sweet but there's an underlying coldness in her tone. "I need to know your intentions with my daughter and now my grandchild."

My stomach sinks and a wave of nausea washes over me. I swear, if the floor could open up and swallow me whole right now, I would feel a lot better. I quickly step to August, grabbing his wrist again as I begin to lead him up the stairs with me.

"Another time, Mother." My voice is strained but I stare at her, my eyes wide as I silently plead for her to just let it go. "He's here to help me study and then I need to try and get some sleep."

"Very well." She nods as she looks back at August. "Next time."

August smiles at her, completely unaffected by her subtle intimidation. "It was nice meeting you," he tells her, oozing charm, and I want to punch him in the chest. My mother disappears down the hall and my feet move quickly as I pull August along behind me, leading him into my room before shutting the door behind him.

"She seems nice," he says as he walks deeper into my room, his eyes scanning my space. I watch him carefully as he walks over to my bed and drops down onto the mattress. "Next time when I'm here and she wants to talk, let me talk to her, Poppy. I need her to know that I have nothing but good intentions behind what's going on between us."

My heart pounds erratically in my chest, my throat constricting around the emotion that builds inside me. These damn pregnancy hormones are seriously getting so annoying. The tears prick at the corners of my eyes, but I swallow back the emotions and nod, before sitting down on the bed next to him.

"Fine," I agree, grabbing my binder and the paper that I thought I had lost that has my notes.

"You can talk to her, but now you're going to help me study."

August chuckles, the sound rumbling in his chest as it warms my body. Pulling my feet onto the bed, I tuck them underneath me and hand August the paper as he begins to look over it. He told me he wasn't good at math, but as soon as he begins to explain things, I can tell he wasn't being fully honest.

He breaks down the methods to solving the problems, explaining them in a way that makes more sense to me and I'm so grateful he showed up. If he wasn't here teaching me this stuff, I'm pretty positive I would be failing the test tomorrow. We fall into a comfortable silence as I work on some of the practice problems that he finds in my book for me.

After finishing them, I hand the paper back to him, his fingertips brushing against mine as he takes it from me. His eyes scan the problems and I watch the way his eyes move, studying his features. He has a face that is almost perfect, except for a small scar just above his eyebrow. I trail my eyes down his perfectly straight nose and sharp jawline.

"Poppy?" August's voice breaks through my staring and I snap my gaze back to his. A storm brews in his irises and a heat creeps up my neck, spreading across my cheeks as a ghost of a smile plays on his lips. "Did you hear a word I said or were you too distracted?"

I swallow hard over the emotion lodged in my throat and shake my head. "Sorry," I croak out, my voice hoarse. "I was just zoning out."

He chuckles softly, his eyes still glued to mine. "I said you got all of them right. I think you have it down and should have no problem with your test tomorrow, as long as you follow the method I taught you."

"Thanks, August," I tell him softly, not fully trusting my voice with the way he's staring at me. "Seriously, you have no idea. I was pretty positive I was going to fail tomorrow, but thanks to you, I feel like I can do it."

"Don't ever doubt yourself, Poppy," he breathes, his voice barely audible as he reaches out to brush a strand of hair away from my face. "You're unlike anyone I've ever met and I don't think there's anything that can stop you from achieving greatness."

A nervous laugh falls from my lips, my skin tingling from where his fingertips brushed against my skin. "If one of us is going to achieve greatness, it's definitely going to be you."

"Stop," he commands, his voice stern as he shifts on the bed, scooting closer as he closes the distance between us. His hands find the sides of my face, gently cupping my cheeks as his eyes bounce back and forth between mine. "Look at everything you've done so far in life, Poppy. You're graduating in, like, three months and that's a whole-ass year early. You're determined and driven, a woman who doesn't need anyone."

"Yeah, right," I roll my eyes, ignoring the warmth building in the pit of my stomach as he strokes the sides of my face. Fuck these hormones and fuck him for making me feel right now. "I'm so strong and independent, living at my parents' house."

"You're here so you can save money and finish your degree, right?" He pauses for a moment, his eyes trained on mine. "Move in with me and let me take care of you."

"Absolutely not," I growl at him, my eyebrows pinching together. "I am more than capable of taking care of myself."

August's lips curl upward. "That's exactly what I mean," he breathes, his gaze dropping down to my lips. "A strong and independent woman who doesn't need a man. And fuck, it's sexy as hell."

I swallow roughly over the lump that forms in my throat and find myself closing the space between us as August brings his face down to mine. He stops, his breath warm on my lips, smelling faintly like candy.

"Fuck, Poppy." He inhales sharply. "I'm going to kiss you and if you don't want me to, now is your chance to stop—"

My lips crash into his, silencing him with my mouth. August groans, his body relaxing as he holds the sides of my face, his lips moving against mine. He feels just like I remember, tender and gentle, as our mouths melt together. His tongue slides along the seam of mine, parting them as he slips inside.

Opening my mouth wider, I let him in as he deepens the kiss, his tongue sliding against mine before tangling together. He breathes me in and I let him drain the oxygen from my lungs as he kisses me senseless. This is purely lust driving, thanks to these stupid hormones and the things that August Whitley does to my body. I don't fight against the moment, letting him sweep me away as I wrap my arms around the back of his neck.

The sound of a door closing down the hallway breaks through the silence and interrupts my lust-driven haze. Abruptly, I pull away from him, my hands falling from his neck. August releases the sides of my face, a smile touching his plump lips as his eyes focus on mine.

"We can't do this, August," I breathe, my chest heaving as I struggle to come up for air. My head is still swimming from the lack of oxygen and drunk on the taste of his tongue. "We're friends and nothing more."

August tilts his head to the side with a crooked grin on his face. "Friends that just so happen to be having a baby together..."

My jaw clenches and my body tingles from his touch, still riding the high of feeling his lips against mine again. "Friends. That's the keyword, baby or not."

"And I wasn't lying when I said that I will be the best friend you've ever had."

I'm already fighting a losing battle, but I can't give in to his charm, to the thrill and the lust of feeling him close to me. This can't happen. I can't let this happen. I have to keep him at arm's length, while still having him around so he's involved. How the hell am I going to do this for the rest of my life, because we're tethered together by a child that will never let that string fray.

"I have an appointment in two days. Come with me?"

August's face softens and the smile on his lips is like a blow directly to my chest.

"I wouldn't miss it."

CHAPTER NINE
AUGUST

I haven't seen Poppy since I kissed her when I was supposed to be helping her study. In my defense, I told her that I was going to kiss her and I gave her an out. If my brain remembers correctly, it was actually her whose lips collided with mine first.

Either way, she's almost been more distant since that moment and I've been mentally beating myself up since. I should have known making a move would spook her, but I couldn't resist her. Fuck, it's so hard being around her and knowing we can't be more than this. I need to work on this friends thing, but I don't even know where to begin.

Poppy's texts and phone calls have been short the past few days, but I've been trying to give her some space. She extended an olive branch, even after we kissed, and invited me along to an appointment. She made it clear that it wasn't one with an ultrasound, so I wouldn't get to see the baby. Just a routine exam for them to make sure she's measuring correctly and to listen to the baby's heart.

Either way, she really didn't have to include me in this appointment if she didn't want to, but she did. And I meant it when I told her that I wouldn't miss this appointment. It still doesn't feel real, but hearing the heartbeat... my brain can't even comprehend the thought.

Poppy is waiting outside of her house, her pregnant stomach covered by her thick winter coat as she strides over to my car and hops in. She tried to argue with me about it, but I insisted on driving her. Anything that I can do to lighten her load—even if she doesn't want my help, she's fucking getting it.

"Hey," she says softly, a smile on her lips as she climbs into the passenger seat of the car. I watch her as she pulls the seat belt across her body, strapping herself in. "Thanks for picking me up."

"Of course," I tell her, pulling away from the curb after she's situated in her seat. "I figured that if I drove, it would be harder for you to turn me down when I ask you to get dinner with me after the appointment."

Her head whips to the side and I can feel her glare on the side of my face. I continue to stare out the window, a smile playing on my lips as I focus on the road. "You're impossible," she mutters, shaking her head as she turns away from me. "You know how hard it is for a pregnant chick to turn down food?"

A chuckle rumbles in my chest as I pull the car out onto the freeway. "I was hoping that'd work to my advantage too."

Poppy laughs and the sound is like music to my ears as it fucks my eardrums in the best way possible. She relaxes in her seat and it brings me a sense of joy, knowing she's comfortable with me. That's all I want... for her to feel safe and like she can let her guard down.

And maybe at the same time, she can let me in.

The drive to the doctor's office isn't far and before I know it, we're pulling into a parking spot and walking into the building together. Poppy leads the way and I fall into step behind her, following after as she leads me into the office. She steps up to the front desk and I hang back, finding a seat as she checks in for her appointment.

The waiting room is empty and I'm thankful for that because I feel like I could break out into a sweat at any given moment. The anxiety and nervousness never really fully hit me until this moment. Today I get to hear my baby's heartbeat and nothing solidifies its life more than that.

Poppy finds me over by the windows and sits down in the seat next to mine. I glance over at her, my nostrils flaring, chest rising as I inhale deeply, attempting to calm my nerves. Her eyes bounce back and forth between mine, her brows drawing together slightly. "Are you okay? You don't look so well."

I swallow roughly, giving her a small smile. "I'm good. Just fucking nervous."

"It will be okay," she assures me, her voice soft and gentle as she places her hand on top of mine. "What are you nervous for?"

Instinctively, I turn my hand over, her palm soft and warm against mine as I lace my fingers through hers. "This just makes it more real, you know? I don't know how to explain it."

"Are you having second thoughts about this?" she asks, just as the nurse pops out through the doorway and calls her name. Poppy goes to pull her hand from mine, rising to her feet, but I don't let go of her as I stand up too.

"Never," I swear, shaking my head as I squeeze her hand.

Her eyes drop down to our hands linked together before finding my gaze. A wave of emotion passes through her deep blue irises and I'm lost for a moment, caught up in the waves as they crash against the shore in the depths of her ocean. The nurse clears her throat, interrupting us with a smile on her face as we begin to walk toward her.

Poppy and I follow her down the hall, to where she stops to weigh Poppy, and we head into the exam room. Poppy climbs onto the table in the center of the room where the nurse checks her vital signs and asks her how things have been going. Poppy relays to her that everything has been going well and as normal as to be expected.

The nurse glances over at me. "And who do we have with us today?"

"That's August," Poppy smiles, her bright blue eyes touching mine. "He's the father."

I watch the nurse as she grabs some receiver-looking thing with a wand and squirts some lube onto it. She walks over to Poppy as she pulls up her shirt and exposes her round stomach. The nurse looks over at me, a smile forming on her lips. "You ready to hear baby's heartbeat, Dad?"

My heart skips a beat, my breath catching in my throat as I walk over beside Poppy and take her hand in mine. "I've never been more ready."

Poppy smiles up at me, her eyes scanning my face as I direct my attention to the nurse as she presses the wand against Poppy's stomach and moves it around. She pauses for a moment, a rapid whooshing sound coming through the receiver she holds in her hand.

"There it is. There's baby's heartbeat and it sounds perfect."

My heart swells, growing three times its normal size, and tears prick the corners of my eyes as I meet Poppy's gaze. Her expression is soft, her eyes warm as she stares at me with so much fucking emotion on her face, I want to kiss it away.

Finding out that Poppy was pregnant was a shock and something I wasn't prepared for. Hell, I still don't know if I'm prepared to be a father, but this—this changes everything. Hearing the baby's heartbeat makes this real and I can't imagine things being any different right now.

Except for one thing... but I'll get to that eventually.

We finish up at the doctor's office and Poppy makes her next follow-up appointment, handing me a card with the date and time in case I want to go along. Which, hell yes. I won't be missing any more appointments with her. I'm really in this—and deep.

I let Poppy pick the restaurant we end up at, since I've heard pregnant women tend to have different cravings for food. I'm not a picky person, so whatever makes her happy is good with me. She picks an Italian restaurant, since she told me that pasta has been her go-to lately.

"Thank you for coming with me today," she tells me after we place our orders and the server disappears. "I know this is still probably a lot for you to adjust to, but it was nice having you come along."

I stare back at her, deep into the oceanic depths of her eyes. "I told you, I'm all in, Poppy." I pause, a smirk forming on my lips. "Even if we are just friends, I want to be as involved in the pregnancy and the baby's life as possible."

Poppy smiles back at me, the emotion welling in her eyes as she takes a sip of her water. "You know, if I'm being honest, I was afraid of having to do this alone. It's not that I was doubting my ability to, but after growing up with divorced parents, I swore I never wanted that for my children if I ever had any. Knowing that you want to be a part of its life brings me more comfort than I could ever explain."

My heart fractures for her, at the thought of her having to grow up like that. It's something that I would never be able to understand, after coming from a home where my parents were together and were the perfect role models for what a happy marriage should look like.

I hate the thought of how she must have felt, planning on doing this alone and the fear she had of me not wanting to be involved. I'll admit, I was shocked at first, but walking away from this was never an option. The moment I knew about her being pregnant, I was locked in.

Poppy doesn't want anything between us, other than being friends, and I respect her decision. I am okay with that, as long as she lets me be a part of her life. But that doesn't mean I don't want more. And even though it pains me to admit it, I want there to be strings, instead of none attached.

I want more of her. I want all of her, in every aspect of my life.

"So, I know you're not really into sports, but I

have a game this weekend and I was wondering if you would want to come."

Poppy tilts her head to the side, a smile curling on her lips. "I would love to come and watch you play." She pauses for a moment, taking a sip of her water as her eyes search mine. "You've never asked me to come before…"

My throat bobs. She's right, I never asked her because before, all we were was a fling. She was someone to occupy my time and distract me from the monotony of life. But everything has changed since we were in that place. She's more than that now.

A nervousness fills me under her gaze and I shrug, attempting to brush it off. "I never thought you would want to before, but since we're friends, I thought maybe you'd want to come."

"Friends…" She chuckles lightly, her eyes bright as her smile touches them. "I would love to, August."

We're just friends.

I can't push her past that point because if I do, I'm afraid I might lose her forever.

CHAPTER TEN
POPPY

Tonight's the night of August's game and I'm more nervous than I had anticipated. I was surprised when he asked me if I wanted to come, especially since he never had before, but things are different between us now. Even if we aren't together, our connection is growing deeper as our child continues to grow in my stomach. Something shifted, that took what was between us from just a fling to a bond that will last a lifetime.

And maybe it's because we both know we will be in each other's lives now for the rest of our days. Having a baby together really changes things and it's almost as if he wants me around more now, like he wants to actually have some type of a bond or relationship, even if it's supposed to remain platonic.

August told me where I would be sitting and gave me the tickets that their team had reserved for the family of the players. He assured me that his sister, Isla, would wait for me near the main entrance too, so she could show me where to sit. I had only seen her once before and am now regretting never introducing myself. When she showed up at the bar with August and his friend, we had just broken things off.

The last thing I wanted in that moment was to meet his damn family.

A sigh slips from my lips as I tug my beanie down over my ears and duck my head against the harsh wind and walk toward the front doors of the arena. I show my ticket to a man standing by the door and he scans it before waving me through. As I make my way inside, I hear someone call my name and find Isla walking toward me from where she was standing against the wall.

Isla strides over to me with a bright smile on her lips and her hazel eyes shining. My eyes nervously bounce back and forth between hers and it's like I'm staring at a replica of August. It's eerie, how much they look alike. There's no denying the fact that they are siblings.

"Poppy." She smiles as she abruptly pulls me in for a hug. It takes me by surprise, but I return her embrace. "It's so nice to finally meet you," she tells me as she releases me and takes a step back. "I mean, I remember seeing you at the bar and I've heard a lot about you, but I'm glad we're finally able to actually meet."

I smile back at her, a light laughter falling from my lips as Isla rambles for a moment. She cringes and sighs in defeat with herself. "It's nice to meet you too."

"I guess I could have just said that, huh?" She rolls her eyes, her lips curling upward as she chuckles and begins to walk toward one of the food stands. "Sorry. Sometimes when I get nervous, I do that."

"It's okay," I tell her, smiling as I follow after her and we get in line. "I get it, trust me. I think we all do it sometimes. But, I promise you don't have to be nervous around me. I'm pretty laid-back and easygoing."

"You'd have to be to deal with my brother," Isla chuckles as we get into line. "I hope you're hungry. They have some pretty good food here."

"Girl, I'm always hungry lately," I tell her, the words just falling from my lips without any warning or ability to hold them back. I would imagine that she already knows I'm pregnant and even though I have my huge winter coat on, my stomach still protrudes a little from underneath it. It's still an awkward subject to approach with August's sister, especially since this is the first time I'm meeting her.

Isla glances over at me, emotion welling in her eyes, and she smiles at me. "I can only imagine."

We both fall into a comfortable silence as we order our food and grab it after paying and head to our seats. Even though it's a college arena, they still have decent seating and we sit in one of the box seats. Isla takes a seat and I sit down next to her, holding my food on my lap.

"When does the game start?" I ask her as we watch the guys skating around on the ice and it looks like they're just warming up. It's the first hockey game I've ever been to and honestly, sports weren't something we ever really watched in my house growing up. Evie was always into swimming and I did track in high school, but that's about as athletic as our family got.

My stepfather, Benjamin, wasn't really keen on sports, preferring to watch more educational things on TV instead. My biological father always enjoyed baseball, but he never really included Evie and I in it. It was like it was his own thing to watch alone. Come to think of it, I don't recall a hockey game ever even being on the television as a kid.

"They should be finishing up their warm-ups any minute," she says after swallowing a mouthful of fries. "There's August," she tells me, pointing out at the ice to the number 19 jersey with Whitley in bold white letters across the back. She then points to another player, number 5 that says Knight on the back of his black jersey. "That's my boyfriend, Logan."

"I heard the two of you were together," I offer, attempting to switch the conversation as I take a sip of my bottle of water. "How did that happen? He's August's best friend, right? I used to see him at the bar a lot with August and met him a few times."

Isla chuckles softly as her eyes find him on the ice, following after him as he skates around, effortlessly tossing the puck to one of the other players. "We knew each other since we were kids. I swear, I was in love with him as soon as I had any interest in boys. It just kind of happened, but it didn't actually happen until after I moved in with the two of them.

We tried to stop it because he is my brother's best friend, but it was impossible."

"Oh jeez," I tell her, letting out an exaggerated sigh as she glances over to me. "I can't even imagine. I'm guessing August didn't take it very well?"

"Not at first," she winces, frowning slightly. "He wasn't exactly in a good place after you disappeared and then when he saw Logan and I kiss one night, everything came out and he beat the shit out of Logan. It's a long story, but he eventually came around to the idea and gave us his blessing. I think he knew that regardless of everything, we would always find our way back to each other. I think he was finally able to see that we are the best for each other."

I smile at her, happy for them being able to find their way back to each other and having August be okay with it. I can't help but feel the twinge in my chest, my heart clinging to her words. August wasn't in a good place after I disappeared. "I never meant to hurt August," I tell her, my voice barely audible as her eyes search mine. "Things were getting complicated between us and we decided our arrangement wasn't going to work. And then I found out I was pregnant... I couldn't face him after that."

"I get it," she says, her voice soft and warm as

she reaches out to squeeze my hand. "All that matters is the future now. You two found your way back to each other, and even if it's just for the baby, I'm glad you're back in his life."

Tears prick the corners of my eyes and I swallow roughly over the lump forming in my throat as I smile at her. Someone whistles loudly and we both glance around, attempting to find the source of the sound as our eyes end up out on the ice. August and Logan are standing side by side at the center of the rink, facing us. They both lift their hands to wave to us, Logan blowing Isla a kiss.

The ref blows the whistle and the announcer begins speaking as all of the players line up on the ice, taking their positions.

"You guys are so sweet," I tell her, a smile on my face as I sit forward a little bit in my seat to see what's happening on the ice below. "Seriously. I know I don't know you, but from what I know of Logan, he's a good guy. And if your brother approves, then I'm sure you two are perfect for each other."

Isla smiles, glancing at me before looking back at the ice as the puck drops. I watch in amazement, completely confused as August slaps at the puck, but he doesn't get it as the other team steals it away and whisks it toward the net. "Do you want me to explain anything that's going on?"

I laugh lightly, shaking my head. "You can if you want, but with this damn pregnancy brain, I don't know how much of it I'm going to retain."

"Well, even if you and August aren't together, you're going to be around him for a long-ass time. The sport will grow on you over time and don't be surprised when he starts saying stuff to you about the game, like constantly." She pauses, her face lighting up as she laughs. "Seriously. I obviously don't play hockey, and he used to have me critique his games for him."

"Oh no," I laugh along with her. "I hope he doesn't expect that from me because I have no idea what to even tell him."

Isla's eyes bounce back and forth between mine. "Stick around and you'll learn the game. He'll teach you and you'll know what to tell him."

We both turn our attention back to the game, Isla screaming at the guys as they skate back and forth fighting for the puck before scoring a goal. She jumps to her feet as a loud horn sounds and she's yelling out proudly at her brother scoring. I'm still a little lost, but I set my food down on the seat next to me and rise to my feet with her in celebration.

I don't understand what's going on, but the longer the game goes on, I start to pick up some of the lingo as she leans over to explain different penalties and shots to me. The way they set up on the ice when the ref drops the puck. It's a lot to take in, but the game is exhilarating, and learning August's world makes my heart swell.

The first period is over and they begin to clear off the ice as the players disappear back into the locker room. Isla turns in her seat, a smile creeping onto her face as her hazel eyes meet mine. "Okay, so when do we find out what you're having?"

A smile falls on my lips and I shrug my shoulders. "I have my twenty-week anatomy scan next, and we can find out then, but the doctors called yesterday and asked if I wanted to do a 3D ultrasound when they do it. So, I'm just waiting to find out when I can schedule it."

"Oh my god, I am so excited, you have no idea!" she practically squeals, clapping her hands as tears well in her eyes. "I can't believe I'm actually going to be an aunt. We have so much to plan! Please tell me we can do a gender reveal? And do you need help with a baby shower? I can totally help plan that."

Panic instantly floods my system. "My mom mentioned a baby shower, but I haven't really thought much about it. I've just kind of been going through the motions of life, but things have been so different now that I know August wants to be involved."

"Well, please let me be involved too," she says softly, her eyes pleading. "And our family would love to be involved and meet you too. August just told our mother and she's coming next weekend, if you wouldn't mind meeting her. We can do dinner at our apartment?" She pauses for a moment, her gaze scanning my face. "If that's not too much for you?"

Inhaling deeply, I attempt to calm my nerves at the thought of all of this happening so soon. It was one thing adjusting to the thought of being pregnant and having a baby, but I never really put much thought into August's family being involved. Of course they would want to be involved.

"What if I ask my mom about doing dinner at her house?" I offer, smiling at her with a warmth passing over my expression. "We can just get it all over with, having both families completely meet. She would love to meet you and your parents and since she only met August in passing, I know she wants to get to know him a little better."

"That would be amazing!" Isla exclaims, flashing her straight white teeth at me. "I'll give you my number and you can let me know as soon as you talk to her and we can figure everything out." She pauses for a moment, smiling at me coyly. "About the gender reveal, though… can we please do that?"

An exaggerated sigh falls from my lips and I can't fight the smile that creeps back onto my lips. "Fine, you can do it. How do you find out without me knowing?"

"Okay, so my cousin did one, like, last summer," she tells me, glancing at the ice as all the players enter the arena again. "When you go for your anatomy scan, tell the ultrasound tech that you don't want to know and ask her to write it down on a piece of paper and put it in an envelope. Just get that from her and then give it to me."

"I think I can do that."

"Perfect," she nods, grinning as she looks back to the game and starts yelling again. I laugh along, listening to her commentary as we watch together. The rest of the game flies by and it's honestly one of the better nights I've had in a long time.

I realize at this moment that it's okay to open your heart and your circle. Isla is a good person, just like her brother. And I want to let her in too. After all, she is going to be our baby's aunt.

The game finishes up and we rise from our seats,

heading back into the hallway area. "You drove here separately?" Isla asks me as we go out to the parking lot.

"Yeah," I tell her, pulling my hood up over my head to block the harsh wind. "August said he didn't want me to be uncomfortable, sitting in the stands while waiting for them to get ready and warm up and everything, since they had to be here early."

I watch as Isla's face transforms, a wave of emotion passing through her eyes, and she stares back at me with a ghost of a smile playing on her lips. "What?"

"He's got it bad for you, Poppy," she says quietly, shaking her head as her smile grows. "He won't admit it, but give him some time and you'll see."

A lump forms in my throat and I struggle to swallow over it. We had a new arrangement, that we were just friends. So far, we've been able to stick to that, but the lines have blurred a little bit... a few times, to be exact.

"We're just friends, Isla," I remind her as she walks me over to my car. "We both want to be here for the baby and have agreed that's all we can agree to right now."

"Whatever you say," she says with a wink, a

smirk on her lips. "Give it some time. That friend shit never lasts... trust me, I know."

Isla gives me a quick hug, reminding me to text her after talking to my mom, before she walks across the lot to her car. I get into mine, turning on the engine and the heat, because it's cold as hell in here. I pull out my phone and send August a message, telling him to call me later. He had mentioned going out after the game, but right now, I just want to crawl into bed and rest.

I make it back to my house, checking my phone once more before slipping into the hot bathtub. August didn't send me a message back, but he's probably busy with whatever they do after the game. I slip into the hot water, soothing my muscles and warming my body from the cold outside. Losing track of time, I stay in the bathtub until the water grows cold.

Stepping out, I grab a towel and dry off, before slipping into my pajamas that I had brought in with me. Just as I let my hair down from the bun I had it in on the top of my head, my phone begins to ring, August's name lighting up the screen.

"Hello?"

"I'm in your driveway," he says softly. "I won't

come in because I know it's late, but I was hoping you would come out and see me."

I swallow roughly, my breath catching in my throat. The butterflies come to life in my stomach, a warmth spreading through my bones. He drove the whole way here to see me since he didn't get to see me after the game.

"I'll be right out."

CHAPTER ELEVEN
AUGUST

I run a hand through my damp hair after hanging up my phone. After the game, I undressed from my gear and slipped into the shower in the locker room without even checking my phone. Poppy and Isla were together after we got off the ice, so I was hoping that maybe they would still be together after the game and Poppy would want to hang out.

When I saw her message after the shower, I instantly felt regret for expecting her to want to hang out after the game. The game wasn't over until close to ten at night and I know how tired she's been lately. I was an asshole for not thinking about her being tired afterward.

I drove over here without thinking, without warning her, hoping she would still be awake. I didn't want to disturb her if she were asleep, but thankfully she sounded like she hadn't been to sleep yet when she answered the phone. I took a chance, driving here just so I could see her for a few minutes because I didn't get to earlier.

And much to my surprise, she willingly agreed to come out and see me.

The things this girl does to me... I may never admit them out loud to her because I don't think we're in a place for that, but for now I will keep it to myself. It was hard to even acknowledge myself, especially when I've been so closed off to the idea of being with someone and having someone come between me and hockey.

But Poppy was different. I couldn't imagine her being with anyone but me. And I might kill any motherfucker I see her with after all of this. She's mine, whether she knows it or not yet. I'll make her see over time, but I need her to come to the realization herself. If there's one thing Poppy needs, it's for her to not feel pressured.

She's too independent to ever rely on someone else and it's almost as if she needs to prove it to herself that she doesn't need me. And to be honest, I like her not needing me. But that doesn't mean I don't want her to want me.

I kill the headlights, leaving the engine running as I sit toward the end of Poppy's driveway. The house is dark except for the light that shines from her bedroom window. I see a shadow pass by it, but no other lights turn on in the house. Watching the house, I wait to see some other sign of life and my heart pounds erratically in my chest at the thought of her not actually coming out.

The anxiety is for no reason, because just as I begin to inhale deeply in an effort to calm myself, the front door opens and Poppy slips out into the darkness of the night. She walks down the driveway, the light above the garage flickering on from her movement, and she picks up the pace as she jogs toward my car.

Unlocking the doors, I lean over the center console and grab the handle for the passenger-side door before pushing it open for her. Poppy is out of breath, rubbing her cold hands together as she drops down into the seat. I reach forward, cranking up the heat, feeling its warmth as it pumps hot air out through the vents.

"Shit, it's cold as hell tonight," she murmurs, pulling her hood up over her head. She turns sideways in her seat, disapproval on her face as she scans my body. "Where is your coat, August Whitley? And you really went out into the arctic temperatures with a wet head?"

"Chill out, Mom," I chuckle, shaking my head at her. "I'm a big boy, I can take care of myself."

Her face softens as she rolls her eyes with a smirk playing on her lips. "That's debatable."

We fall into a comfortable silence for a few moments, her eyes nervously bouncing back and forth between mine as she rubs her hands together in front of the vent that continues to blow out hot air. Her face is free of any makeup and she looks so innocent and young. I can't fight the smile that tugs at the corners of my lips as I lose myself in her beauty.

"Why are you here, August?" She asks softly, nothing menacing behind her tone, only pure curiosity.

My tongue darts out, nervously wetting my lips. "I just wanted to see you since I didn't get to after the game."

A frown forms on her plump lips and regret fills

her eyes. "I'm sorry. I had a great time at the game and hanging out with your sister. I was just really tired after such a long day and honestly, I just wanted to come home and relax."

"You don't have to explain yourself to me, baby," I tell her, the word falling from my lips before I can stop it from happening. Her eyes widen slightly, a pink tint spreading across her cheeks, but I don't falter even though I fucked up. "I only want you to worry about taking care of yourself and the baby. I want you healthy and feeling good. If you're too tired to do something or just want to relax, then you deserve that."

Her eyes stare directly through mine, straight through my fucking soul. "When did you turn into such a sweet person, August Whitley?" Her voice is quiet, as if she's actually taken aback by my words. "I'm not saying that you were an asshole before, but you've changed—and it's not a bad thing."

"Or maybe it's because you're finally getting to know me."

Poppy's face softens, a ghost of a smile on her lips as she tilts her head to the side. "I'm not finished getting to know you. We're just getting started."

Her words hit me directly in the core and I can feel her under my skin, spreading through my system like a slow-killing poison. She's fatal to my fucking soul and if she continues to situate herself in my bone marrow, in every fiber of my being, I would die happy.

Taking a chance, I inch closer to her, reaching out for the side of her face as I bring her closer to me. Poppy doesn't object, meeting me halfway as her lips softly press against mine. She tastes like mint and her lips feel like silk, gliding against mine as I move my mouth against hers. Her hands slide across my shoulders and she's pushing me back against my seat as she climbs over the center console, settling on my lap.

Her nails dig into my shoulders as she clings to me. Pushing down her hood, my hands slide around the back of her head and my fingertips slip between her long locks of hair, holding her close to me as I consume her with my mouth, stealing the air from her lungs. My tongue swipes along the seam of her lips and she instantly parts them, letting me in as we melt together.

Our tongues tangle together and she feels like coming home, her in my lap with her nails biting into my shoulders. Releasing her head with one hand, I slide it down her torso, reaching for the bottom hem of her sweatshirt. Slowly lifting it up, I slip my hand under her shirt, feeling her soft, supple skin beneath my palm.

Poppy moans into my mouth, her hips shifting as she grinds herself against me and I continue to stroke her skin, moving my hand farther up her torso. My cock is hard underneath her, straining against my sweatpants as she moves on top of me. My balls constrict, a warmth spreading through the pit of my stomach as I lose myself in her.

Our movements are faster, fueled by lust as our mouths move together, my lips bruising hers. It becomes more urgent, no longer gentle as I need to feel closer to her. I fucking need her more than words could ever describe and we're too caught up in the moment to come to our senses.

Her hands travel down my chest, reaching for the bottom of my sweatshirt. She slides her hands underneath, pushing my shirt up my stomach as she runs her fingertips across my body with featherlight touches. She breaks away for a moment, her hooded gaze searching mine as she reaches for her own shirt.

I press the button along the side of my seat, lowering the back down as my eyes meet hers, watching her as she peels off her sweatshirt and t-shirt in one swift movement. She lifts them over her head, tossing her shirts onto the other seat. My gaze drops down to her body, my hands running over her swollen stomach, pausing for a moment as my eyes desperately search hers.

"You look so fucking sexy right now, baby..." My voice is hoarse, filled with need as my cock pulsates in my pants. "Sitting here in my lap, my baby growing in your stomach. Fuck..."

My fingertips slide under the wire of her bra as I look to her for permission. Her lips part slightly, a soft breath slipping from them as she reaches behind her back and unhooks the clasp of her bra. Reaching for her, I grab the straps from her shoulders and slowly slide them down her arms before releasing her breasts.

I slide my hands underneath them, cupping them in my palms. They're swollen and full, her nipples erect from the need that is driving both of us.

Poppy tugs on my arms, pulling me forward as she reaches for my shirt. "Your turn."

A soft chuckle falls from my lips and I follow her

command, stripping my shirt off before discarding it with hers on the other seat. She runs her hands over the planes of my stomach and chest, feeling the muscles between her palms. My cock is painfully hard and I need to be inside her right now. I don't want to push her, though. This is already a step past friendship, the lines blurring the closer we get.

Grabbing the back of her neck, I pull her flush against me, her breasts crushing against my chest as I claim her mouth with mine again. Poppy continues to touch me, her fingertips lightly caressing my skin as she slides her hands across my chest and shoulders. I can't get enough of this fucking girl and she knows it.

She runs her hands down my torso, reaching for the waistband of my pants as her tongue slides against mine, tasting me. I slide my palms along her back, resting along her lower back as I press her against me, craving the friction of feeling her grinding against my cock. She rolls her hips, a moan falling from her mouth, and I swallow her sounds as she continues to move against me.

"Fuck, baby," I breathe against her lips as she breaks away for a moment. "I want you so fucking badly."

She slides her fingertips underneath the waistband of my pants, slowly stroking my skin with her featherlike touches. I pull her face back to mine, our mouths colliding as I feel the warmth spreading through my entire body. I can't take this, having her so close, yet I don't know if this is what she really wants.

Poppy would have stopped me if she didn't want this, but at the same time, we're so driven by our emotions and the tension between us that has been building. I told her I would be the best friend she's ever had, but I can't help but feel like maybe I'm taking advantage of the situation.

"Is this what you want, baby?" I ask her as I pull away, my eyes searching hers. "You want me to fuck you in my car right now? Because all you have to say is yes and I will."

It's almost as if reality slaps her in the face and I watch the color drain from her cheeks. "Oh my god," she whispers, her eyes widening as she quickly covers her chest. "I am so sorry. I don't know what came over me. We can't be doing this."

"Says who?"

She narrows her eyes at me, grabbing her bra from the seat as she quickly puts it back on and grabs her shirt. "We're supposed to just be friends, August. Friends don't do this kind of shit."

"Fuck the friendship."

Poppy shakes her head, pulling her shirts over her head as she abruptly climbs off my lap and into the passenger seat. "I'm sorry, August. I don't know what came over me, but I'm sorry for that happening."

"Don't apologize, Poppy. It's fine, seriously. It was my fault, not yours. I shouldn't have come here and bothered you."

She wrings her hands together before reaching for the handle as she opens the door. "I'll call you, okay? I'm sorry, but we can't do this."

My face falls, but I quickly recover, offering her a soft smile. "Don't apologize, please. And I'll be waiting for your call." I pause for a second, watching her as she climbs out of my car. "Get some sleep, Poppy. And if you dream of me, don't be afraid to touch yourself."

A pink tint spreads across her cheeks. "Goodnight, August."

A chuckle falls from my lips and I wait until she's in the house before backing out of the driveway. I don't turn on my headlights until I'm on the street, and my cock is still hard in my pants as thoughts of her in my lap play over my head.

Goddamn this girl and the things she does to me...

I'm ready to fuck up our friendship and take things to the next level.

I just need to figure out how I can make her mine...

CHAPTER TWELVE
POPPY

It's been four days since August showed up in my driveway the night after his game. Four days since I practically attacked him like an animal in heat and climbed onto his lap, exposing half of my body for him to see. It's not like it's nothing he's never seen before, but it was completely out of line for me to act like that.

The lines get blurred when I'm around August and the more time we spend together, the more it seems like they completely vanish. I love getting to know him better, on a deeper, more personal level, but at the same time it doesn't feel like it's working in my favor.

We agreed to just being friends and navigating how to co-parent together. That didn't mean we had to devote our lives to each other. Instead, we were devoting them to our child, but the closer we get, the more I feel strings beginning to form. And we agreed there would be none attached.

He's had my head a mess and I don't know what to do with these feelings that have begun to resurface. I thought I could ignore them, but I'm afraid I can't anymore, even with the distance I've been trying to keep between us.

August hasn't brought up that night, but every morning when I wake up, there's already a text waiting for me from him, wishing me a good day. He texts me throughout the day, making sure I'm okay and whether I need anything. And then our days end with goodnight messages.

I've successfully avoided talking to him on the phone since the night he showed up after his game. He hasn't come out and questioned me on it, but why would he? I'm pregnant, so it's only natural that I would be exhausted at the end of the day, especially being in an accelerated program at school. I'm so close to the finish line for my degree and I've been pushing harder than I have the past three years I've been attending college.

August has been so attentive, it's almost strange, but I'm slowly coming around to realizing that he really does care. On a level I haven't quite figured out, he cares about me and not just solely because of the baby.

It's probably a conversation we should have soon, but it's one I don't know how to approach or even have the mental capacity to face right now. Who's to say that it isn't just the pregnancy hormones anyway? My emotions have been a wreck and I feel like I can't fully trust them. Do I really have feelings for him or is it because I'm pregnant?

What happens when the baby comes and the feeling disappears? What if it's the same for him? He hasn't come out and said anything to me regarding how he feels about me or the prospect of us pursuing something other than being friends, but he's made his comments that have implied as much.

What if after the baby is born, he doesn't feel the same way about me anymore?

Shaking my head to myself, I'm brought back to reality as my professor steps in front of my seat and taps on my desk with her pen. I look up at her, my eyes wide as I realize that I've been zoning out, completely consumed by the thoughts that plague my mind and I didn't even notice that class was over and everyone had cleared out of the room until now.

"Are you okay, Poppy?" she questions me, her

voice soft as she sits down in the seat in front of me. "I noticed that it seemed like I lost you there toward the end of the lecture and then when you didn't get up when class was over, I was a little worried."

A nervous chuckle slips from my lips and I quickly collect my notebooks, shoving them into my bag with my pen. "I'm fine. Just a little tired and sometimes my mind wanders when my body is ready for me to take a nap."

"I know this all must be a lot on you." Her eyes are warm, with a wave of sympathy passing through them. "I just want you to know that a lot of people in your position wouldn't be making such an effort like you are to complete all of your classes on time still."

"If I can get them done and out of the way, I'll be able to graduate before the baby arrives."

She smiles at me as she rises to her feet, pushing the chair back in. "I just wanted you to know that your hard work and dedication don't go unnoticed. I'm proud of you, Poppy. But don't forget to take care of yourself too, okay?"

I nod at her, following suit as I stand up from my seat and collect my stuff. "Thanks, Professor Rheems. I've been doing all right so far, but I really do appreciate your kind words."

"If you ever need anything, don't hesitate to ask," she offers as she walks toward the front of the lecture hall to her desk. "Personal disclosure—I had my daughter at a young age too. I know it's not easy, so even if you just want to talk sometime, I'm here to listen."

"I appreciate that," I smile at her as I head toward the door. "Have a good day!"

She waves to me and I glance at my phone as I make my way down the hall. August sent me a text, and I don't understand how he finds the time to bother me all day long when he's supposed to be in classes himself. I don't bother questioning him on it, though, because if he weren't on top of his class work, he wouldn't be allowed to play on the hockey team.

As I walk down the steps to the foyer of the building, I unlock my phone and open his message, a smile touching my lips as my eyes scan over his words.

AUGUST

> How's your morning going? Is the baby ready for you to eat lunch yet, because I found a place that isn't far from campus that is supposed to have banging Italian food and I just so happen to be in the area.

Laughing to myself, I shake my head at him, even though he can't see me. Leave it to August to find a way to insert himself into my day. He's lucky I don't have another class for about two hours, and pasta just so happens to be my kryptonite right now.

POPPY

That sounds amazing! You're seriously my hero. I just finished class, so send me the name of the restaurant and I'll meet you there.

The glass doors slide open and I step out into the sunshine, feeling the warmth on my skin that is a stark contrast to the brisk chill in the air. I shiver, wrapping my coat tighter around my body as I tuck my phone into my pocket. As I lift my head and start walking toward the parking lot, I see August's car parked alongside the curb out front.

He's standing on the sidewalk, his hands loosely tucked in the front pockets of his joggers as he leans back against the passenger-side door of his car. As he sees me, I watch his lips curl upward into a grin and he pulls his sunglasses away from his face, pushing off the car as he stands up straight.

Walking over to him, I can't fight the grin that forms on my face, the chuckle that slips from my lips as I roll my eyes at him. "Of course, you're already here."

"Always, baby," he replies softly, pulling open the door for me. He takes my bag from my arm as I lower myself into the seat and he closes the door behind me.

I watch him as he walks around the front of the car, heading over to the driver's side with my bag slung over his shoulder. My stomach flips, my heart already in my throat as my mouth grows dry. The last time I was in his car, I ended up half naked in his lap... and I'd be lying if I said that I didn't want that to happen again.

Get it together, Poppy.

Until we have an actual talk, I need to remain firm in our decision to just be friends. It's not my fault he has the effect on me like he does. And for the record, I didn't ask him to come pick me up. That doesn't mean I'm not allowed to be a little excited about it. Even though I was the one trying to put distance between the two of us.

"So, you ready to go get your fill of pasta?" August smirks as he climbs in behind the wheel and tosses my bag into the back seat. He puts his sunglasses back over his eyes as he shifts the car into drive.

"I swear, you know the way to my heart."

The words fall from my lips before I have the chance to stop them and I instantly want to take them back. A heat creeps up my neck, spreading across my cheeks in embarrassment. August glances over at me, the smirk no longer on his face, and I can't see his eyes through the black shades covering them.

"That's the plan, Poppy," he murmurs, pulling the car out onto the street as he directs his gaze back onto the road. "Your heart is the finish line."

I swallow hard over the lump forming in my throat, my hand instinctively going to my stomach as I glance out the window. The tension hangs heavily in the air between us, his words swirling around like wisps of smoke. I want to reach out and grab them and store them in my heart for later, but something tells me I don't need to.

Words like that will forever be imprinted in my brain.

With my hand over my stomach, I feel something weird inside, almost like my insides are rolling. I press my palm against one of the firmer parts and I feel a flutter, something hitting my hand. A gasp falls from my lips and I jerk my head to the side, looking at August with my eyes wide. "Oh my god, August."

"What?" he says, pushing up his sunglasses as he brakes at a red light. His hazel eyes desperately search mine, laced with worry. "What's wrong? Are you okay?"

A sob catches in my throat and I nod as I grab his hand and hold it against my stomach. His eyebrows tug together, his gaze still trained on mine as I hold his palm to my abdomen where I felt the movement. I feel the rolling sensation again and something pressing outward.

"What was that?" he whispers, his voice barely audible, almost like he thinks something is still wrong. The light turns green, but he doesn't dare move the car, despite the cars honking their horns behind us.

My lips curl upward, tears instantly springing to my eyes as a quiet laugh escapes me. "That was our baby kicking, August."

His throat bobs as he swallows hard, his nostrils flaring as his eyes wash over with moisture. "Oh my god…"

I smile back at him, knowing the exact feeling he's feeling right now. It's one thing seeing your baby during an ultrasound and hearing the baby's heartbeat, but it's a completely different experience feeling them moving around inside.

It was both of our first times and I wouldn't have wanted either of us to experience this amazing moment without the other.

This is what I really want with him…

Every goddamn moment.

CHAPTER THIRTEEN
AUGUST

Holy shit.

I just felt our baby move for the first time and judging by the look on Poppy's face, I think it's her first time too. She never mentioned feeling it before and she's told me everything that has happened so far during the pregnancy. She showed me the ultrasound pictures she had from her first one, where the baby still looked like a blob... and that moment didn't come close to comparison with this one.

Another car blares it's horn behind us, completely ruining the moment, and I let out an exasperated sigh. "Fuck," I mumble as the moment is ruined and I pull my hand away from Poppy's stomach, giving the driver behind me the middle finger. "Fucking asshole."

Poppy laughs, glancing over at me as she wipes the tears away from her cheeks. "Calm down, August. You'll get to feel it again. That was just the first and from what I've read, it only gets more frequent and more intense the further along I get."

I feel like compared to her, I know nothing about pregnancies or babies. Maybe I should get some books of my own to read and try to catch up.

Stepping on the gas, I flash a smile at her. "Okay, okay. Sorry, I just hated that the moment was interrupted, you know?"

"I mean, we were sitting at a green light instead of moving." She smiles back at me, shaking her head as she looks back out the window. "Plus, there will be more moments."

"That's what I'm counting on," I tell her, my voice soft and quiet, but loud enough for her to hear. With the way her body tenses and the sharp intake of her breath, I know she heard what I said.

Poppy doesn't say anything back to me, but I wasn't looking for a response from her. Her body betrays her every single time, telling me exactly what I need to know, confirming my suspicions. The other night wasn't just a fluke thing fueled by hormones and lust. It was so much more and she may not come out and admit it, but she's not feeling this friend thing either.

We're both silent as we cover the short distance to the restaurant, the soft sound of the radio playing in the background that takes up some of the space in the car. I wasn't actually in the area, like I told Poppy. She told me before that she gets a break around lunchtime and since she's been avoiding me, I wanted to surprise her.

There's nothing wrong with two friends getting lunch.

Even if one of the friends wants to be more... so much more.

It's a quaint little Italian restaurant that I found when I googled places near her campus. It's in a small town, tucked away like a little hole-in-the-wall. There's an empty spot directly out front of the building and I pull in, putting the car in park before killing the engine. I quickly hop out and race around to Poppy's door, pulling it open before she gets a chance.

"Thanks," she says quietly, her voice shy as she looks up at me through her long black lashes. My eyes fall to her plump lips as she pulls the bottom one between her teeth and in this moment, I want to kiss her. To sweep her off her feet and devour her, like a starved man.

As we step into the small restaurant, the deep aromas of the food that they're cooking has my mouth instantly watering. Poppy looks up at me, her gaze bashful as she shifts her weight nervously on her feet. The host quickly arrives in front of us, grabbing two menus before leading us to a table tucked away in the corner of the dining room.

"I like it here," Poppy muses, her eyes scanning the dim room with elegant decor. "I've never been here before and it smells divine."

Sitting across from Poppy, I watch her as she looks around the room almost in amazement. From the way the restaurant looked from the outside, the inside is much different than either of us were expecting. Almost like whatever this is between Poppy and I. At the start, from the outside, it never looked like much, but once you open the doors and step inside, it's like nothing you've ever experienced before.

I order both of us water, knowing Poppy has been on a kick with drinking mainly water lately, and she gives me a shy smile as she knows that I've clearly been doing my homework and paying attention. If there's one thing I can't take my attention away from, it's her.

Jesus, it really is her... and I've been too stupid and blind to realize it sooner.

It's always been her.

"So, what do you think you're going to order?" Poppy asks me as her eyes scan the menu before she closes it and sets it on the table in front of her.

"I think I might try the lasagna," I answer her, mimicking her actions as I set the menu down on top of hers. "What about you?"

Poppy's face lights up, her lips curling upward. "Spaghetti, no meat."

I laugh lightly, shaking my head at her predictability. "Is that the only thing that you eat anymore? I swear that every time we get food or I ask you what you're eating, it's spaghetti and plain-ass sauce."

"Hey." She glares at me playfully, her tone scolding. "I can't control the cravings, and apparently this baby is a pasta connoisseur or something."

We're both laughing, the mood light and there's no heaviness or tension between us as the server arrives back at the table with our waters. We both give him our order, thanking him for the drinks before he disappears back toward the kitchen to put in our food order. Poppy's eyes trail around the restaurant again before they land on mine, a soft smile on her lips as her laughter dissipates.

"August," she says softly, my name rolling off her tongue, and I want to taste it. Her deep blue eyes are focused on mine, the waves lightly crashing against the shore, and I want to drown in their depths. "I have a question and I don't want to ruin things between us, but I have to know. You don't have to answer if you don't want to, but I at least want you to be honest."

I nod slowly, swallowing hard over the knives that are suddenly lodged in my throat. "Nothing but the truth, Poppy."

She pauses for a moment, her nostrils flaring as she exhales deeply and takes a sip of her water. I watch as she carefully sets the glass back down on the table in front of her and wipes the condensation away from it with her fingertips as she focuses back on me. "What are we doing? I know we agreed on being friends, but it doesn't feel like that's what this is anymore..."

"That's because it isn't," I admit, the honesty oozing from my words and I'm unable to take them back as soon as they leave my lips. Poppy's eyes widen slightly, but I don't stop. I can't stop now or

I'm going to fuck it all up. "We're more than friends, Poppy. And it's not just because we're having a baby together."

Her eyes bounce back and forth between mine, her body stilling, her hands wrapped tightly around her glass of water. "What are we doing, though?"

"You want the honest answer?"

She nods, her throat bobbing as she swallows. I watch her for a moment as she lifts the glass back up to her lips and takes a long sip. "Please."

"I don't know what the fuck we're doing," I breathe, shaking my head as a smirk plays on my lips. "Honestly, we've been avoiding the inevitable, pretending we could just be friends. Tell me, baby. Did you really think it would ever work out?"

Her eyes are still wide, but they stop searching mine as she stares straight through me and I feel her burrowing herself into my bones, wrapping herself inside my marrow. "No," she whispers, shaking her head. "I just hoped it would."

Tilting my head to the side, I lift an eyebrow in question. "Why?"

"Because, I don't know if I can survive your destruction. And the thought of being together scares me. Relying on someone else… I don't want to lose myself in the process. What if things end? What happens then? It would be fucking messy, especially with a baby involved."

My eyebrows pull together and I fold my arms over the top of the other on the table. "So, what? We keep pretending and leave things the way they are to avoid getting hurt? You think life isn't going to be messy with a baby if we're not together from the start?"

"No. I don't know," she says quietly, her eyes full of emotion as she stares back at me. "I just don't know, August. I obviously like you and we'd both be lying if we said there wasn't anything between us. I just need some time, okay?"

I nod, the sound of her voice cracking tugs at my heartstrings and I want to reach across the table and pull her into my arms. She asked for my honesty, she wanted to know what we were doing here, and I'm not sure I gave her the answer she wanted to hear. She can't deny that this friends thing isn't working out, though.

My heart tells me that it's all or nothing, but I can't not have her in my life. Even if she just wants to be friends, I'll be whatever the fuck she wants me to be.

CHAPTER FOURTEEN
POPPY

I don't know what answer I was really looking for from August, but his response still threw me off. In a way, I was surprised. I asked him for his honest answer and when he laid it all out there, it was almost like a punch to the gut. We've both been trying so hard to make this friend thing work out and now I know I'm not the only one who is struggling.

I think part of me wanted him to say he wanted to just be friends and didn't want to pursue anything else between us. That maybe it was just the lust and the hormones between us that had us unable to keep our hands off one another when we were alone and the tension was high.

Instead, he told me that we've both been

pretending and screw him for hitting the nail on the head. I wish what he said wasn't true, but it is. We really are pretending and the closer we get, the worse we get at this charade.

And here I lay, at almost midnight, alone in bed, still replaying our conversation from earlier in the day over and over in my head.

Sleep should have found me long ago, especially with how exhausted I was after the day, but it's as if my mind was refusing to let me go to sleep with this still lingering. I couldn't give him an answer then and I still don't think I could now.

He dropped me off back at campus after we had lunch and promised he would give me space. He said he would wait for me to reach out to him when I was ready and I could tell it pained him just to utter those words. I can still picture the pain washing over his eyes as he stared back at me as it began to drizzle in the dreary afternoon.

I couldn't stop thinking about it. It consumed my every thought during the rest of my classes and after I got home. My mom could tell something was on my mind when we all had dinner, but Benjamin told her to let me be when she attempted to question me. I silently thanked him, because sometimes it was as if my stepfather knew what I needed when my mother was being overbearing.

After retiring early to my bedroom, I took another hot bath in an attempt to calm my heart and soul, but it failed. Nothing seemed to help right now and I kept checking my phone as if I were expecting a message or a phone call from August, even though he had promised me he would give me space.

I shouldn't reach out to him, but a part of me feels desperate to talk to him right now. This is what he does to me. Somehow he has a way of fucking with every part of my brain and I can't get him out regardless of how hard I try. For once, I just want some peace, but my heart won't let me have it, not when it feels like it's missing the vital piece it needs to beat.

Rolling onto my side, my stomach protrudes a little more than normal and I feel the same fluttering inside that I did earlier today. A gasp slips from my lips and I press my hand against my abdomen, feeling for another kick. It's a small one, just like when I was with August, but it's still there. Our little miracle—the unexpected thing that came from us being together and one thing I would never do over.

It's almost as if it's a sign. August is going to be a part of my life for the rest of my days, whether things work out between us or not. Would it really hurt to try? To try and at least make things work for ourselves, not even just for the baby. We both deserve that chance and sometimes there are risks in life that you have to take, even if it feels like it's too big of a gamble.

And as much as it scares me, as much as I loathe gambling, I think it's time I roll the dice. How much could it possibly hurt? The worst thing that would happen is one of us would end up with a broken heart and I'd be willing to bet it would be me before it would be him. I think I'm at the point where I'm ready to take that risk, to put everything on the line and see what happens...

Even if he does hurt me in the end.

Reaching over to my nightstand, I grab my phone and unlock the screen before I go to my messages. I know it's late and August is probably asleep, but I can't help myself. Sometimes there are things you need to get out, regardless of the time of day. And even if he doesn't read it until the morning, at least I know I said what I needed to say.

The thought of calling him passes through my mind, but I quickly push it away, opening the last messaging thread between us instead. I don't know whether I can handle hearing his voice right now or it might derail my plans of how I want to go about this.

> POPPY
>
> I've been thinking after this afternoon… and you were right, August. We've been pretending this whole time and it's not working anymore. I can't be your friend. I want to be more than that.

I wait for a moment, staring at the screen, but nothing happens. It says at the bottom corner of my message that it was delivered, but I figure that August is probably asleep, like I should be. A sigh slips from my lips and I lock the screen, setting it back down on my nightstand as I tuck my hands back under my pillow and nestle my head into it. Pulling the covers back up to my chin, I bury myself underneath.

Closing my eyes, I block out the soft light glowing from my night-light across my room. Yeah, I'm an adult and still sleep with a night-light. When I had my own apartment, I slept with the TV on every night. It was more out of habit than comfort. Since I moved back in with my parents, I never got around to hooking the thing up in here, so I've been sleeping with a night-light and an easy listening playlist on my Spotify account that I have on my phone.

Focusing on my breathing, I attempt to push the lingering thoughts of August from my brain. Inhaling deeply, I count and hold my breath before exhaling for another few counts. I feel it as it begins to slow my heart rate down and my body begins to relax deeper into the bed. August's face still doesn't leave my mind, but it makes it easier—the only thing that has made me feel somewhat relaxed since we had our conversation over lunch earlier.

My phone suddenly vibrates, startling me. I peel my eyelids open, my heart pounding erratically in its cage as if the breathing exercises I just did didn't mean anything anymore. My breath catches in my throat as I lean back over and pull my phone into my hand from the nightstand and pull it closer to me.

Unlocking the screen, I see a message with August's name on it. A smile touches my lips as the anxiety runs through my system. He was the one who said we weren't just pretending and he wanted more from me, so I don't know why I'm nervous. What I said to him is basically wanting the same thing he said to me. But what if he changed his mind since we last talked? I wouldn't blame him if he did. Not only is having a baby a huge commitment, but so is being with someone.

AUGUST

> Baby, baby, baby... You really mean that?

The smile on my lips spreads further, a grin completely consuming my face as I laugh lightly. Emotion clogs my throat and tears prick the corners of my eyes. I'm relieved and elated at his message. I hope I didn't wake him up from sleeping, but I'm thankful he responded. That he read my message and knows what I want—that I want the same things he does.

POPPY

> More than anything, but I only have one condition.

I don't bother closing my phone, staring at the message thread and the three small bubbles popping up as he quickly responds. They don't go away and come back, instead they disappear as his message comes through immediately.

AUGUST

> Lol, you and your conditions, Poppy Williams.

A laugh falls from my lips again and I bury myself under the covers, feeling like a little kid with a first crush as I hold my phone under with me, typing back to him. The butterflies spring to life in my stomach, scraping my insides with their wings, and I love the feeling spreading through my body. The effect August has on me...

POPPY

> I want to take things slow. I don't want to rush into anything, even though we both know we've always been more than friends and have clearly had sex before. I just want to go slow and make sure this is what we both really want.

I swallow hard over the emotion in my throat. I know this is what I really want, but what if it isn't what he wants? Or he could change his mind at any given time. I always knew that if I had kids, I didn't want them to come from a broken home like I did with my parents. I have more faith in August than I did in my real father.

As much as I want to believe that he wouldn't do

the same things my father did, it's hard to tell what someone will do. You think you know someone and then they turn around and prove that you really didn't know them all along. I know how much hockey means to August—how that comes first in his life and always has.

But will it always come first? Having a baby changes everything and I need him to understand and realize that. I would never be the one to come between him and the sport he loves, the sport he's working so hard to turn into a career. But I need to know where his priorities lay, because if it comes down to it, I will choose the baby and its well-being over him.

A child needs at least one reliable parent and if August can't be that, I will have to be the one that makes that choice, even if it breaks me in the process. The only thing I can hope for is that it never comes down to that.

AUGUST

> We can take things as slow as you want, baby. You know I would never pressure you or force you into something you don't feel comfortable with. You're more important to me than I would ever be able to explain and I just want you to give me the chance to prove that to you. Let me show you how I really feel about you, baby. No more of this being friends bullshit.

I stare at his message, my heart crawling into my throat as it restricts my airway, and I swallow hard over the emotion building inside me. Three small bubbles pop up again before I get the chance to respond.

AUGUST

> Be mine, Poppy. Let's make it official. You're my baby momma, but I want everyone to know that you're my girl. My girlfriend.

The emotion has me choked up, my heart pounding erratically in its cage as I reread his message over and over again. I wanted to tell him how I was feeling, that I wanted to be more than friends as well.

And he wants me to be his.

POPPY

I'm yours, boyfriend.

My stomach does a flip as I type out the words and send the message.

AUGUST

You always have been, baby.

CHAPTER FIFTEEN
AUGUST

This feels surreal.

I know Poppy wants to take it slow and I am more than happy to do that with her. All I want is a chance to see where this goes between us. I know she has her reservations but I need to show her that I meant every word I said, that I am worthy of her love and her time. She's afraid of what will come in the future, but we can't worry about that now. We have all the time in the world to get to where I want us to be.

Poppy has had a heavy week of classes and studying, but I've managed to get her to go to lunch with me every day so far. This week we've been swamped with practice in the evenings, on top of studying, so in a way it was better for our week to be spent in fleeting times together.

Soft kisses and light touching. Nothing too heavy or enough to make this go faster than she wants. The ball is in Poppy's court and I'm following her lead when it comes to what she wants. The guys have been on my case about not spending time with the team like they'd like.

When it comes to those guys, we're like family, like a brotherhood. So much of our time has been spent together, but there comes a time where I have to make time for other things in life, not just them. I tried explaining to Poppy that I can't keep her hidden for long, especially when they know we've made things official.

They all want to meet the mother of the child the team is no doubt going to adopt as their own. Our little one is going to have plenty of uncles to go around and the thought alone makes my heart swell.

It's the weekend, game time, and I feel jacked and ready to go. When I asked Poppy to come, she looked like she was going to burst at the seams with happiness. And it made my heart sing. I don't like asking so much of her because I know it's a big commitment on top of everything else going on in her life, but knowing that she'll be in the stands watching is like another shot of adrenaline to my system.

Isla offered to drive her, since the game isn't at our arena tonight, and I was thankful for that. The last thing I wanted was for Poppy to drive two hours to see me play, and it was a chance for her to spend time with my sister. She was more than happy to oblige, and Isla expressed how much she likes Poppy and wants to get to know her better.

Plus, according to Isla, Poppy is going to let her plan the gender reveal party.

The entire team got a hotel for the night, so none of us have to drive back, and Poppy agreed to stay with me. With it being a late game and long drive, it made the most sense. We're heading home after we check-out of our room to have dinner at Poppy's house with our parents. They wanted to come to the game tonight, but I didn't want them to have to make the drive out here, since it was five hours away from their house.

They weren't exactly happy about it, but understood where I was coming from. They agreed to stay home this weekend and would make sure to put in their travel plans to come to the first regional tournament game instead. We still have another month until those games start, but we're starting to get more into a playoff mode with the way we've been playing.

I know I have their support, even if they're watching our games from home. That's enough for me. They're two people who have been more supportive than a kid could ever want their parents to be and I'll forever be grateful and in their debt for it. They're already driving to Poppy's parents' tomorrow for dinner and that's enough of a drive for them.

I can't focus on that right now. I met Poppy's mother in passing, but I want her to know that my intentions with her daughter are clear. And to finally meet her stepfather, who is more present in her life than her biological father. Poppy and Isla figured it would be best to have our parents come too, because that way both families can meet—and I need my parents to meet Poppy.

She's too important to me for them to not know her.

I glance up at the stands once more, my eyes finding Poppy before I get into my stance for the face-off. My eyes meet my opponent's and he cuts them at me for a moment before I drop my gaze back down to the ice, waiting for the puck to drop.

The ref drops it down between both of our sticks and it's a fight to win the face-off. He slaps his stick against mine, trying to take the puck away from me, but I manage to work it away from him, slapping it back toward our defense. I lift my head, skating toward center ice as I look back and see Logan with the puck.

He skates with it for a few moments before sending it flying across the ice to Cam. He's already anticipating Logan's pass and stops the puck with the blade of his stick effortlessly. I skate forward as he stickhandles it, keeping it with him as he flies past the other team's defense as they begin to come toward us on a mission.

This isn't a playoff game, necessarily, but every game matters right now in the season. We're already sitting in the first seat for the regional championship with the most points in the league, but that doesn't mean every team isn't trying to get their spot in the bracket too.

The team we're playing has been one of our biggest contenders this year and they just so happen to be the team Logan has gotten into the most fights with. If we can keep him out of the penalty box tonight, that alone will be a win. It's always beneficial to have an enforcer who likes to get shit done, but sometimes he takes things a little too far.

He's the protector of our team and if any one of the opposing players does one of ours dirty, Logan is going to be coming for them and he's not going to stop until he's the last one standing on the ice.

Hayden skates toward the net and Cam lifts his head, looking for someone to pass the puck to. The other team's defense is on me, knowing I play center so I would be the most likely candidate to pass to in an attempt to score a goal. Hayden's open and Cam passes it to him before the other team gets the chance to interfere.

Their defense falls back, skating to defend the goal as their goalie gets into position. Hayden takes a shot, but it's deflected by their goaltender, bouncing off his shin pads before it goes sliding back toward center ice. Spinning around, I start heading back down the ice and see Logan as he gets it when it comes into his zone.

He passes it over to Sterling just as someone calls shift change from the bench. My legs are already burning, my chest rising and falling in rapid succession. Cam and I skate toward the bench, hopping over the boards as Simon and Liam take our places, skating out into their positions.

Sitting on the bench, I squirt some water into my mouth, watching as the other team steals the puck and takes it down toward our net. Asher, our goalie, is already in place, his eyes following the puck like his life depends on it. They attempt to make a clear shot, but Logan blocks it before it gets to Asher. He slaps it back toward center ice, where Hayden is already skating toward, and he presses harder, taking the puck down the ice with him.

One of our other defenders calls shift change and Logan and Sterling come skating over to the bench as two more guys head out and take their places. Hayden should be coming back, but he's practically open right now, skating like a fucking madman toward the net. He stickhandles the puck, faking out the goalie who drops down to the ice just as Hayden sends it flying into the top shelf.

We all jump to our feet as the horn blares throughout the arena and we're all yelling, slapping our sticks on the boards. Hayden skates around, everyone tapping his helmet with their gloves or fist bumping him with the bulky covering on their hands. He skates over to the bench as one of our freshman players, Vaughn, hops the boards and skates out.

"Shit, I missed playing with you guys," Hayden

tells Logan and I as he squirts some water in his mouth. "You have no idea how good it feels to be back with you two."

Logan laughs, bumping his shoulder against Hayden's and I smile at him, nodding. It's almost like old times and I didn't realize how much I missed having him around. He's definitely been an addition to our team that won't do us wrong and I think our coach can see that, especially with this being his debut game on our team.

The game continues on and we all go through our various shift changes, effectively scoring one more goal before the period ends. The other team managed to sneak one past Asher and it was a bit of a dirty play that had Logan on edge.

We're all sitting, catching our breaths as we wait for them to clean the ice before we go back out for the second period, and I see Logan staring at the floor in the locker room, his mind somewhere else. Things have been good with him and Isla and looking back now, I can make the connection that the problems between them is what really fueled his anger.

"Dude, you need to chill out," I tell Logan as I make my way over to him. "It was a dirty play, but it wasn't a dirty hit. Go out there with a clear head instead of trying to start shit."

Hayden walks over on his skates, sitting on the bench across from us. "Logan still likes to fight, huh?"

Logan lifts his head, glancing between the two of us. "You know how I don't like that shit. Seriously. Don't fuck with our players or you're going to get fucked with back."

"Knight," Cam interjects as he leans against the locker and pulls his helmet over his head. "We don't need you in the penalty box again, okay? If it's a dirty hit, I fully support you going after them. Let this one go, though, all right? We're too close to the end of the season for this shit now."

Logan sighs, rolling his eyes dramatically at all of us. "Fine, but if I agree to this, you're all buying my beers tonight."

"Deal," Cam says, extending his hand to Logan, and they shake on it.

Our coach pops his head in, calling for all of us to head back out to the ice, and we all strap on our helmets and head back down the tunnel toward the ice. We're all in a single file line and Hayden walks behind me, tapping on my shoulder as we get closer to the rink.

"I'd be willing to bet that Logan ends up fighting someone anyways."

A sigh slips from my lips and I look back at him through the visor of my helmet. "Hopefully he doesn't, but I wouldn't be surprised if he does, anyways. He gets a little too protective sometimes and lets his anger get the best of him."

Hayden shrugs as we all skate across the ice toward the bench. "He's our brother, Whitley. You know how we all feel about family."

I look at him as we hop the boards, a smile touching my lips. "You go to war for them…"

CHAPTER SIXTEEN
POPPY

The game ends and August's team wins, scoring the last goal with only thirty seconds left on the clock. It was an intense game to watch, but it was enjoyable. I never thought hockey would be a sport I'd actually enjoy, but there's something about the atmosphere and the adrenaline rush of watching the game.

I would be lying if I said there wasn't a part of me that got nervous watching August out there. The players are ruthless and the way they hit each other and get slammed into the boards, it makes me nervous that he's going to get injured. And falling on the ice like they do... I know they wear pads, but it still has to hurt sometimes.

Isla sighs as we walk out to her car, her shoulders hung in defeat as she pulls open her door and drops down into her seat. I follow, quickly shuffling my feet as the cold air burns my cheeks and I hop into the passenger's seat.

"What's wrong?" I ask her as she turns on the engine and we wait for it to heat up. The vents blow out cold air at first before switching to hot air as she cranks up the heat.

Isla glances over at me, checking the time on her phone before she drops it into the cupholder and puts the car in reverse. "Logan is supposed to be working on his anger and not fighting as much. He managed to get through the last game without hitting someone, but obviously that didn't happen tonight."

I purse my lips, frowning as I give her a sympathetic look. It's one thing to be worried about August getting injured just playing the game, but it's another thing to be worried when there's fighting involved. And I've seen Logan fight other players out there and he's pretty vicious.

"He doesn't seem like an angry person," I offer, shaking my head almost in disbelief. "He's not like that with you, is he?"

"Oh, God no," she says, a light chuckle falling from her lips. "Are you kidding? Do you really think that my brother would let him live if that were the case? When August first found out about the two of us, he beat Logan up and it was pretty bad." She pauses for a moment, chewing on the inside of her lip as she pulls the car around the back of the building to where the players' entrance is. "I honestly don't fully understand his anger. I think part of it has to do with his father walking out on him when he was a baby and this is where he gets the aggression out. I don't know, I don't like to bring it up if I don't have to."

"Doesn't it worry you, though?" I question her as we sit in the darkness, waiting for the guys to come out. "Him fighting like that... what if he got seriously hurt?"

"Of course. Sometimes I hate watching him play because I never know what's going to happen." She pauses, turning in her seat to face me. "Earlier this season, he took a pretty bad hit and was knocked out. He suffered from a really bad concussion and I was so fucking scared. He couldn't play for a few weeks, but as soon as he was cleared, he was back on the ice."

A gasp slips from my lips and my throat constricts. I know people get injured in sports all the time, but I can't even imagine how she must have felt when that happened. I don't know what I would do if it were August.

"There's one thing you need to understand if you're going to be with my brother, Poppy," Isla says quietly, her eyes bouncing back and forth as they search mine. "Hockey is a part of them. It runs through their veins. Nothing will ever stop them from playing, unless they get seriously injured or die. It sucks to think about, but it's the reality. Without hockey, I don't know who they would really even be. It's just something you have to accept as part of your life now, but if it's too much, don't be afraid to worry about yourself."

I've known from the start that hockey will always come first for August, but after hearing it from Isla, it solidifies it and I'm not sure how I feel about that. We have a baby coming... his priorities should change. The baby should come first.

"It's only going to get more intense too, after college when he starts to play professionally." Isla's eyes are sympathetic, but she needs me to hear this, to fully understand. "Our father played professionally and he missed both of our births. There were a lot of birthdays, parties, vacations that he ended up missing because he had games. Just know what you're getting into, Poppy. You have to think about you and the baby too."

Staring back at her, my voice is caught in my throat and I'm not sure how to respond. She doesn't say the words with any malice or a threatening warning. Instead, she's just offering insight for what to look forward to in the future. The thought alone shakes up my head and I feel like I can't see straight.

Isla falls silent, her attention directed toward the building as we watch the guys start to file out. They're all laughing, each of them appearing in good spirits as they pull their bags behind them, hockey sticks in hand. August is the third to last to come out, walking alongside Logan as they talk about something. He lifts his eyes, his gaze finding mine through the windshield of the car and I watch as a smile touches his lips when he sees me waiting for him.

The other guys all head to their own cars in the parking lot and Isla pops the trunk as Logan and August load their stuff into the car and hop into the back seat. Both of them are freshly showered and the smell of their soap fills the space around us as they laugh about whatever they were discussing before getting in.

"Hey, baby." August's voice is soft as he leans

forward, his hands finding me from around the back of the seat. I put my hands over his forearms as he wraps them around me, his head sliding forward as he presses his lips to my cheek. "I hope you guys weren't waiting too long."

Logan reaches out to touch Isla, but there's an awkwardness between them as she looks at him with a wave of disappointment falling over her expression. I hear Logan sigh and he disappears back into the back seat, no doubt recoiling from Isla's coldness toward him. I can't say that I blame her, especially when Logan isn't supposed to be fighting and he just got into another fight during the game tonight.

"As if you guys could ever be fast enough in the locker room," Isla mumbles, rolling her eyes as she puts the car in drive. "I don't know what you guys could possibly be bullshitting about in there, but I swear, you take forever every time."

Logan chuckles, apparently not too affected by Isla's attitude toward him and August squeezes my arms before falling back into his seat. "You know how it goes, babe," Logan tells Isla as she looks at him through the rearview mirror.

"Unfortunately," she grumbles, her disapproval evident in her voice. "So, where are we going?"

"The guys just want to go to the restaurant and the bar that is at the hotel, if that's okay with you guys," August tells her from the back seat. "I looked at the menu earlier and saw they have some pasta dishes, Poppy."

My heart swells at his words and even though they're just about food, it means so much more than that. He knows how my cravings have been lately and he's been nothing short of accommodating. He took the time to look at the menu, to make sure there would be something that would interest me before deciding on the place. He makes me swoon with one little freaking sentence.

"That works for me," Isla tells him, pulling the car out onto the road as we follow behind some of the other guys. "I'm not trying to stay up too late anyway, since we have to drive back home in the morning."

"I'll drive, baby," Logan offers softly, his voice warm and tender. "I want you to enjoy yourself tonight."

She cuts her eyes at him through the rearview mirror again. "Well, I guess you should have thought about that before you went and did the exact opposite of what we talked about before your game."

I hear August chuckle and I divert my attention back out the window, watching the rows of trees speed past as we head down the road. Well, this is going to be an awkward night. As if I wasn't already nervous to meet the entire team, now the only person I'm actually friends with is pissed off. And August definitely isn't helping with the way he finds her disapproval amusing.

"So, Poppy," the one with curly brown hair, Cam, turns his attention to me as he takes a sip of his beer. "Tell me how someone like you could have possibly ended up with someone like August?"

I choke on my water, quickly recovering as I swallow it down, and all of their eyes are on me. August introduced me to all of the guys as soon as we arrived and got to our large table at the restaurant. I don't like having all of the attention on me, but I'm the new person here, so it's only natural that they're going to question me.

"A lot of alcohol and good tip money," I tell him, winking as the guys all start to laugh. I look over at August, his lips curling upward into an amused grin. "No, he came to the bar and wouldn't leave me alone. And you know how it goes."

Cam laughs, shaking his head. "Whitley, you better not fuck this up or I might have to swoop in and steal your girl. I like her."

August cuts his eyes at him as a shadow passes over his expression. "You even think about it and I'll turn your brain to fucking mush."

"That wouldn't be hard to do, considering he's already practically there," Hayden throws out as he tosses some fries into his mouth. August told me about the guys before I met them and I remember him telling me about Hayden.

He and Logan were best friends with him growing up, so they've known him for a long time. He only just recently transferred to their school and started playing on the team with them again. August didn't mention why he transferred in the middle of their junior year... only that something happened where he last was and his parents were able to get him out of there with a lot of money.

Tilting my head to the side, I study him for a moment. He seems like the rest of them with the whole frat boy persona. He cracks jokes and talks shit, seeming to be pretty laid-back and easygoing. I watched him when they were playing, and although he appeared aggressive, it didn't seem like there was an underlying anger like with Logan.

He's honestly a mystery and I'm curious as to how he ended up here, but it isn't my place to ask. I scan his face, the way his wavy brown hair falls effortlessly across his forehead. His face looks like he's the pretty boy of the team, his cheekbones and jawline defined. As he turns his head to the side, I notice a small scar on his forehead and it piques my curiosity. As his light gray eyes meet mine, he narrows them suspiciously and I quickly divert my gaze elsewhere.

August leans over toward me. "You see something you like?" I don't miss the jealousy in his tone, the way his words bite out at me with venom lingering on the tips of his teeth.

I look over, cutting my eyes at him. "If you're forgetting, your baby is growing in my stomach. I don't have eyes for anyone but you. I was just trying to figure him out and what his story is."

Logan overhears us, chuckling as he leans into our space. "Good luck on that one, because we've known him for a lifetime and still can't figure him out."

"What's so funny, Knight?" Hayden growls at

him, smacking the table lightly. "You guys talking shit or something? Let the rest of us hear it."

Logan narrows his eyes at him from across the table. "Just trying to figure you out still. Why don't you share with the class why you were able to transfer in the middle of the year?"

"Logan, let it go," Isla warns him, her voice low and threatening. "That's Hayden's business and he doesn't have to share it."

"I mean, if he wants to walk around like he's king fucking shit when he's really got a body rotting in his closet, I think we all deserve to know the truth."

"You really want to know why?" Hayden questions him, his eyes cold and hollow. "Everyone wants to know my fucking business? Cool. I fucked the coach's daughter at a party and her jealous friend took a picture and leaked it around campus."

Cam looks over at him, eyes wide. "No fucking way." He looks at him in disbelief. "Please tell me you didn't know it was the coach's daughter before you slept with her."

Hayden tilts his head to the side, a smirk forming on his face. "Oh, no. I knew..."

CHAPTER SEVENTEEN
AUGUST

"Well, that was an interesting dinner," Poppy muses out loud as we step into our room and I lock the door behind us. "Are they always like that?"

Shaking my head, I walk over to her as she sits down on the bed and faces me. "No. But we're all like brothers, so they can be assholes to each other since we spend so much time together."

"Does Logan have a problem with Hayden or something with the way he called him out like that?"

A sigh slips from my lips and I kick off my shoes before I pull my shirt over my head and toss it over toward our suitcase. "No, Logan was just in a weird mood tonight. I don't know what his deal is, but I'm sure Isla will get him straightened out and he'll be apologizing to Hayden tomorrow."

Poppy rises from the bed, walking over to the suitcase as she grabs my shirt and puts it inside. I slip out of my sweatpants, leaving on my boxers as I climb under the covers and lean against the headboard, watching her from across the room.

"Did you mean what you said?" I ask her, my voice quiet with nervousness lingering in my words.

She turns to face me, pulling her shirt over her head, and drops it down into the suitcase. My throat bobs as I swallow, my eyes trailing over her plump breasts covered only by her bra, leading down to her round stomach. "What do you mean?" she asks as she slips her fingers under the waistband of her pants and shimmies out of them.

"That you only have eyes for me..."

Poppy stands across the room by our suitcase with only a bra and lace underwear on as she stares at me. My heart is in my throat, my stomach doing somersaults as her blue eyes meet mine. "You're the only one that I see, August."

"Come here," I growl, my voice husky as I pull back the covers and motion for her to get into the bed. Her lips tip upward and she saunters across the room, looking sexy as hell with her swollen belly and all. Poppy lowers herself onto the edge of the bed, crawling toward me on her hands and knees. Instead of occupying the space beside me, she settles on my lap, straddling me with her toned thighs.

My hands find her hips, gripping her flesh as I hold her on top of me. Poppy plants her palms against my chest, her skin warm against me as she begins to move her fingertips across my pecs. Her eyes search mine and I'm lost in the oceanic depths of her irises as she slides her hands along the sides of my neck before slipping them through my hair.

Her face drops down to mine, her breath soft as it skates across my lips. "You're all I've ever seen, August Whitley. Don't fuck this up."

With one hand on her hip, I wrap the other around the back of her neck, bringing her mouth down to mine as they collide against one another. My lips move against hers, hers mimicking my actions as we melt together. The heat grows between her legs and my cock is already throbbing, pressing against her with just the material of our underwear separating us.

Poppy slides her tongue along the seam of my lips, parting them as her tongue slides against mine, tangling together as they're caught in their own intimate dance. My fingertips dig into her skin, holding her firmly against me, and she moans into my mouth as I draw her bottom lip between my teeth and bite down on it.

I swallow her moans, draining the air from her lungs as I swallow her whole. I can't get enough of her and feeling her here in my lap has me going fucking wild. Without a single drop of alcohol in my system, my head is clearer than it's ever been when we were in bed together in the past and I'm ready to get lost in this moment with her... to effectively lose myself in this girl forever.

Poppy breaks away, coming up for air as she leans back away from me. My hand slides down her torso, the other gripping her hip as she plants her hands back on my chest. Her eyes stare directly through me, seeing straight into my soul as she makes her home inside my heart.

I watch her, my lips parted slightly, bruised from her kiss as she reaches around her back and unclasps her bra. She slowly slides it down her arms before tossing it onto the floor beside the bed. Instinctively, I reach for her, cupping her plump breasts in my palms as she continues to stare down at me.

"What happened to taking things slow?" I

murmur, kneading her flesh within my hands as I take her nipples between my fingers and lightly tug on them.

"We've been going slow enough," she breathes, moaning as she grinds against me. "I'm done with that. I need you and I'm tired of tiptoeing around that."

A soft chuckle rumbles in my chest and I pull Poppy toward me. As she plants her hands on the bed beside my head, I wrap my arms around her waist and swiftly roll her onto her back, following along with her. She inhales sharply as I press my lips along the base of her throat, slowly trailing kisses, nipping and licking her skin until I get to her breasts.

Taking one in my hand, I lift my head, my eyes finding hers. "You got me, baby. Whenever, wherever, your wish is my command. You're embedded under my fucking skin, I'll never be able to get you out."

"Good," she breathes, her lips curling upward as I lower my mouth to her, pulling her nipple between my lips. "Because I'm not going anywhere, ever."

Her head falls backward, her eyes falling shut, and a moan slips from her lips as I swirl my tongue around her pebbled flesh. Drawing it between my teeth, I lightly nip at her skin, kneading her flesh within my fingertips before dragging my tongue across her chest to her other breast.

Poppy lets me take care of her. Her chest rises and falls with each shallow breath as I take my time tasting and teasing her. Sliding my hands down her body, I hook my fingers under the waistband of her panties as I begin to kiss my way down her torso.

Her hands slide through my thick hair and she pushes my head down between her legs as I drag her underwear down her thighs. Her pretty pink pussy is in my face and I spread her legs farther, hooking the backs of her knees over my shoulders as I press my lips to hers.

"Mmmm," she moans, running her hands through my hair. "Don't stop, August."

A chuckle slips from my lips and the sound vibrates against her flesh as I drag my tongue along her center. Poppy's hips buck, thrusting her wet pussy in my face as I begin to feast upon her. She tastes sweet and I moan against her, circling my tongue around her clit. Working my lips against her, I alternate between licking and sucking her, swirling around the tender bundle of nerves that drives her fucking crazy.

Her hands grip my hair and she holds my head

in place, her hips bucking as I fuck her with my mouth. I can tell she's close with the way her legs tighten around my head. Using my hands, I peel them away from my head, pinning them to the bed as I work my mouth and tongue against her, driving her closer and closer to the edge.

"Oh my god," she cries out, losing herself as her orgasm tears through her body. Her grip tightens on my hair, her hips bucking involuntarily as her legs begin to shake. She fights against me, attempting to move them from my grip, but I keep them spread open as I lick her, tasting every fucking drop.

She's breathless, her face flushed, and she looks so goddamn beautiful. A smile forms on my lips as I lift myself from between her legs and she watches me with a euphoric, hooded gaze. As I crawl back over the top of her, her hands are already reaching for my boxers, attempting to pull them down. Moving my hands over hers, I push them out of the way and peel my underwear from my body before tossing them onto the floor.

"I need to get a condom," I tell her as the thought enters my head. It's just a habit, almost like second nature.

She reaches out to grab me, wrapping her delicate hands around my arms as I attempt to move off the bed. "Why? You can't get me pregnant twice."

"Are you sure?" I ask her, my eyes bouncing back and forth between hers. I know I can't get her pregnant since she already is, but I don't want her to feel uncomfortable or anything.

"Well, actually," she pauses, narrowing her eyes at me. "It depends on whether or not you've been with anyone else. Are you clean?"

I stare down at her, a smirk playing on my lips. "Baby, baby, baby," I murmur, brushing a piece of hair from her face. "I haven't been with anyone but you since you came into my life."

Her eyes widen slightly, her lips parting as a wave of emotion passes through her eyes. "Don't you dare lie to me, August Whitley."

"Never, baby," I tell her, my mouth claiming hers. Sliding my tongue along hers, I taste her before breaking apart. "Since the moment I met you, even if I didn't want to admit it at first... it's always been you and it always will be you."

Poppy wraps her hands around the back of my neck, her legs wrapping around my waist as she pulls me back to her. Our mouths collide and I settle between her legs, the tip of my cock pressing against her wet pussy. She urges me forward, nipping at my bottom lip as she pulls my hips down to hers. I slowly slide inside of her, swallowing her moans as I fill her to the brim with my entire length.

This is our first time having sex since she got pregnant and the thought immediately enters my mind and I still against her, pulling away. Planting my hands on either side of her head on the bed, my eyes desperately search hers as panic floods me. "What about the baby?" I begin to panic, attempting to pull out of her, but she locks her legs around my waist. "Poppy, let me go. I don't want to hurt the baby."

I watch as a look of amusement passes over her expression and her eyes crinkle as laughter spills from her lips. She thinks it's fucking hilarious and here I am, freaking the fuck out. "Babe, you're not going to hurt the baby, I promise."

Staring down at her, I shake my head, feeling the embarrassment creeping up my neck before it spreads across my cheeks. "How can you be sure? How do you know it's not going to feel my dick in there or something?"

Poppy bursts out laughing, her chest rising and falling as she struggles to catch her breath and snorts. "Oh my god," she giggles, her eyes filling with tears as she stares up at me. "August. I've read pregnancy books and talked to the doctor. I promise, you have nothing to worry about."

"I don't know if I can do this. We're going to have to wait until after the baby is born or something."

She giggles again, shaking her head at me as she grips the nape of my neck, pulling my face down to hers. "Don't do that to me, please," she pleads, giving me those puppy dog eyes of hers. "I need this between us right now, August. I need to feel you close, filling me like you do."

I swallow hard over the emotion and panic that still wells in my throat. Nodding, I agree, pressing my lips to hers as I let her distract me with her tongue. I slowly slide my cock back inside her, careful to not fill her completely, but she urges me forward with her legs, taking my entire length as I plunge deep inside of her.

It's difficult, shaking the panic that still lingers, but she slides her tongue across mine, her fingertips gripping the back of my neck and I feel her pussy tightening around my cock. A growl slips from my lips and she swallows the sound as she effectively distracts me, completely pushing the thought and panic from my mind.

Lifting away from her, I move her legs away from

my waist and I pull out of her for a moment, the protest already on her lips. She clamps them shut, swallowing her words as I roll her onto her side and lie down on the bed beside her, sliding back inside her from behind. With her back pressed against my front, we spoon and I can feel every inch of her skin.

My hands roam across her body, her arm wrapping around the back of my neck as she twists her body and brings my mouth back down to hers. Our kiss is no longer sweet and tender, instead it's rushed and urgent, her pussy clamping around my cock again.

A warmth spreads across the bottom of my stomach, infiltrating my system as my balls begin to constrict, drawing closer to my body. I slide my hand down to her ass, gripping her cheek in my palm as I begin to slam harder into her.

"Tell me how you want it, baby girl," I breathe against her mouth as she turns her head away from me. Biting at the back of her neck, I drag my tongue along the small half-moon shapes that my teeth leave in her flesh.

"I want you to fuck me, August," she moans, pressing her ass against me as she leans away from me. "I want to feel your balls slapping against me as you fuck me hard."

"You good if I move you onto your hands and knees?" I ask her, gripping her hips as I slow down my thrusts, slowly fucking her.

She glances back at me over her shoulder, her eyes glazed over in pleasure as they meet mine. "Do whatever the fuck you want to me, baby."

Grabbing her hips with both of my hands, I flip her over, lifting her ass in the air, as I follow along with her, my cock still inside her tight pussy. I position myself on my knees behind her and slide my hand along her spine, stopping at the base of her neck as I press her chest down toward the bed.

"Fuck me, August," she breathes, half moaning as I pull my hips back, leaving just the tip inside her. "Fuck me like you mean it."

That's all it takes, her consent, her telling me what she wants, and I plunge back into her, thrusting into her with such force she cries out. For a moment, I'm worried I hurt her, but she presses her ass back against me and I take that as my cue to keep going.

Sliding both of my hands to her ass, I grip her flesh with my fingertips and pounding into her, over and over again, fucking her with no mercy. Poppy takes every thrust, the sounds of our moans and skin on skin slapping filling the room. I can't get enough of her and I'm so close—so fucking close. I slide one hand around the front of her, playing with her clit as I push her closer to the edge.

Her pussy clamps around me, squeezing my cock in a vise grip and I feel her orgasm as it begins to tear through her. She's a fucking mess, losing herself around me as she comes hard. Her legs shake, her pussy convulses, and I'm right there with her.

"Come for me, baby," she moans, pressing her ass back against me again. "I wanna feel you fill me with your cum."

That's all it takes to send me falling over the edge with her, floating into the euphoric abyss. I lose myself inside her, filling her with my cum as I slide into her once more, her pussy taking my full length. Poppy collapses onto the bed as I slowly pull out of her, both of us breathless and still riding the waves of our high.

Poppy struggles to catch her breath as I rise from the bed and slip into the bathroom to grab a washcloth. After running it under some warm water, I bring it back into the room to her, pressing it between her legs as I clean up the mess we made together.

"Jesus Christ, that was amazing," she breathes,

her bliss-filled eyes finding mine as she lifts her head from the pillow.

"You're amazing," I retort, a smile playing on my lips as I clean her up and toss the washcloth over toward the bathroom. Climbing back in the bed, I settle under the covers behind her, wrapping my arm around her waist as I pull her close.

"This is all I want," she whispers, relaxing against me as she laces her fingers with mine. "I want things to always be like this between us."

"And they will, baby," I promise, pressing my lips to her temple. "I'm not going anywhere."

I hold her close, feeling the same exact way she does. I never want this moment to end, it would be so easy for things to always be like this between us, but I think we both know it won't always be this easy. We're adding a baby to the mix, but that won't come between us.

What worries me is everything else in life. I need Poppy by myself and after having her in my life like this, I know I never want to let her go. There is nothing that could possibly come between us that would ever make that happen.

I just hope she feels the same way I do...

Because I'm falling hard for her, and I want her to fall with me.

CHAPTER EIGHTEEN
POPPY

Riding back home the next morning has my stomach in my throat. With August's parents in town, it only made sense to have them come to my parents' house for dinner this evening. My mother was ecstatic. She has been dealing with my pregnant ass for long enough, she's just happy to have everyone else involved. Especially August, even though I know she would like to get to know him better.

I'm nervous to meet his parents, since I've never met them before. And it's a little awkward meeting them now when I'm already pregnant. There's a part of me that wishes I would have had the opportunity to meet them before, but we weren't an exclusive thing then. August wouldn't bring a girl home that he was just messing around with.

From what August has already told me, it seems like he has told them a lot about me. And they already know I'm pregnant and are excited about it. Isla made sure to tell me that their mother is beside herself, already planning their move closer to us, even though their father doesn't want to move.

It warms my heart, knowing our child will have so many people involved in its life that love it. That doesn't calm my nerves at all, though. I won't feel better until after we get the awkwardness of meeting over and hopefully settle into a comfortable conversation. I've never had an issue with first impressions, but it's a little different in this situation.

This isn't just meeting my boyfriend's family... it's meeting the family that will be in my child's life.

"You okay?" August asks, his expression soft as his eyes find mine. He turns to face me, his hand resting on my thigh as we sit in the back seat of Isla's car.

Nodding, I swallow back my anxiety and offer him a small smile. "Just a little nervous for this afternoon."

August's grin spreads across his face, his eyes

lighting up as they stare directly through mine. "You have nothing to worry about, baby," he breathes, his breath warm on my skin as he leans forward and presses his lips to my forehead. "They already love you and haven't met you yet. Trust me when I say you're already part of the family."

Isla glances over her shoulder from the passenger seat, her hand in Logan's as he drives her car down the freeway. "Our mom has been talking nonstop about meeting you, Poppy. Just be prepared, she might be a little overbearing, meeting her golden child's girlfriend."

Logan chokes out a laugh, attempting to cover it up as he forces out a fake cough. August chuckles, shaking his head as he glances at his sister. Her eyes are on his, narrowed with irritation. First it was directed at Logan and now it's toward August. I feel like there's something I'm missing and I hope it doesn't have anything to do with me.

"Don't mind her," August whispers to me, winking as he looks back at his sister with a smile. "Isla's just jealous that I've always been Mom's favorite."

"Bullshit," she mumbles, shaking her head in disapproval. "The only reason you're the favorite is because you just had to follow in Dad's footsteps. If you weren't his little hockey prodigy, they wouldn't have had their worlds centered around yours."

The air in the car is tense and I shift uncomfortably in my seat. A fluttering feeling ripples inside my stomach and I place my hand over it instinctively as I look between August and Isla.

"Whoa," Logan warns Isla, glancing at her as he switches lanes. "Just calm down, babe."

She looks at Logan and sighs, her shoulders sagging as she dials back her irritation. Turning around in her seat, she glances at me, a sympathetic smile on her face. "I'm sorry, Poppy," she says softly, her eyes searching mine. "I've had a lot going on lately between my parents and I, and I didn't mean to take it out on August in front of you like that."

"She's family now, Isla," August interjects, his hand squeezing my thigh. "If you're going to let your bitchy side come out, I think she can take it."

"August. Just shut up?" Logan glances at him through the rearview mirror. "You know your parents aren't thrilled with her decision to major in fine art. You're not exactly helping the situation here."

"You've never dealt with their disappointment," Isla practically whispers, her eyes burning holes through August's. "I've been dealing with it most of my life."

August grows tense beside me for a moment before he releases the breath he was holding. "I'm sorry, Isla," he tells her, his voice soft and gentle. "They're not disappointed in you, they just want to make sure that you're doing what is in your best interest."

"And that has nothing to do with what makes me happy, does it?"

They're caught up in an intense stare-down as the tension in the air grows thicker. It's suffocating and I resist the urge to put down my window to let some oxygen wash it out. There's a tug on my heart and I find myself missing my sister in this moment. I remember the arguments with Evie, the disputes like what August and Isla are having right now.

I wish Evie was here to talk to right now. If she were in the car, she would know exactly what to say to diffuse the situation—to make it less awkward. Evie always knew how to make everyone smile, even when they were having the worst day. That was the charm of her good side, the side of her that wasn't intent on destroying everything.

"You good?" August's voice probes my eardrum, drawing me out of my thoughts as I glance over to him. His eyes search mine with concern, but he doesn't voice it in front of everyone. "I'm sorry if our arguing bothered you."

"You get used to it," Logan offers from the front seat, a soft chuckle falling from his lips. "These two argue like a married couple and then it blows over two seconds later. Just ignore them—that's what I do."

Isla lightly punches his shoulder as August shakes his head, the lilt of his laughter wrapping itself around me. "You're supposed to be on my side, Logan Knight."

"Another tip," Logan tells me, smiling as he pretends to ignore Isla. "Never pick sides when it comes to either of them because the one you don't choose will never let you live it down."

Everyone falls into an easy laughter, the sound filling the car and banishing the awkwardness that hung heavily after their little argument. We continue our journey home with August's hand in mine and the lightness filling my heart. This is how I want things to be—easy—but I know that will never happen... not with August Whitley.

———

We arrive at my parents' house before August and Isla's parents arrive. They called Isla when we were getting closer that they were still an hour out. The thought brought me relief because it gives me some time to prepare to meet them. My mom and August can also get better acquainted before his parents come too.

As we walk into the house, the soft hum from the TV comes from the living room and the aroma of dinner floats down the hall. We all file inside, August carrying my bag from the night with him. He sets it down on the floor by the stairs and everyone kicks off their shoes as my mother comes strolling into the foyer.

"Hey, Mom," I say softly when I see her, and she pauses in front of us, wiping her hands on her apron with a smile on her face. "You remember August. This is his sister, Isla, and her boyfriend, Logan."

My mother smiles at the three of them, extending her hand to shake theirs. "It's so nice to meet the two of you. I'm Claudia."

"It's so nice to meet you," Isla offers, shaking her hand after Logan does. "You have a lovely home and whatever you're making smells amazing."

August steps forward, overshadowing his sister, per usual. "Is there anything we can do to help you?"

I swear, my mother swoons at him before looking over at me. "Come along. I'll put the three of you to work."

Rolling my eyes, a soft laughter falls from my lips as Isla and Logan follow after her into the kitchen. August hangs back with me for a moment, his hand finding the small of my back as we begin to walk through the foyer together.

"I'm going to let your mom give them some jobs and then I want to talk to her, if that's okay with you?"

Swallowing roughly over the emotion and anxiety that wells in my throat, I nod slowly. "What did you want to talk to her about?" My mother already expressed her desire to speak with August, but this is the first time he's said anything about it. He's the one who's taking the initiative.

He pauses just outside the kitchen, his hand finding my arm as he pulls me to a stop and turns me to face him. Towering over me, I have to tilt my head back to look into his eyes and he's staring at me intently. "I want her to know my intentions with you. I've never done this before, but I need her to know that you are safe with me. That I will do everything to take care of you and the baby."

August's hands find the sides of my face and he

gently cups my cheeks, stroking my skin with the pads of his fingers. "Trust me, Poppy. I got you."

Nodding, a smile tugs at the corners of my lips as I pull away from him, sliding my hand into his as we walk into the kitchen. My mom already has Logan washing dishes in the sink and Isla is helping her load different trays into the oven.

August leads me over to the island in the center of the kitchen, his hand leaving mine as he wraps his arm around the top of my shoulders. His lips are soft as he plants a kiss on the side of my head before meeting my mother's gaze across the room.

"Mrs. Vance," he says softly as he pulls away from me and walks closer to her. "Can we talk for a minute?"

"Of course." Her voice is warm and the smile on her lips lights up her eyes. She takes off her apron and hangs it on the back of one of the chairs. "Please, call me Claudia. And let's go talk in the den," she offers, motioning for him to follow her.

I watch as the two of them disappear into the hall and make their way to the den. Isla is watching after them with a look of curiosity in her eyes. "August wants to talk to her about us and the baby. Since she doesn't really know him, he wants to reassure her."

Isla smiles, nodding. "Good," she muses, glancing over at Logan who is also smiling like a proud parent. "It's about time he does the right thing."

Benjamin comes walking into the kitchen and I introduce him to the two of them. He and Logan fall into an easy conversation as he questions Logan about hockey. Benjamin has never been one for hockey, but he knows how to keep the conversation flowing and appears interested in everything Logan tells him.

Just as Isla and I settle on the chairs surrounding the island, the sound of the doorbell ringing echoes through the house. Isla's eyes meet mine, a smile slowly tugging at the corners of her lips.

"I hope you're ready to meet the parents, because they're here."

Smiling back at her, it doesn't quite reach my eyes as my heart pounds anxiously inside my chest. I'm not ready, but there's no better time than the present, right?

CHAPTER NINETEEN
AUGUST

"I wanted to talk to you about Poppy and I," I tell Claudia as we step into the den and she shuts the French doors behind us to give us some privacy. "I know this is all sudden and new, but I want you to know that she is safe with me."

Claudia smiles at me as she stands in the center of the room. "You're right, it is very sudden. I know Poppy didn't tell you about the baby right away and she hasn't told me much about your relationship prior to that, but I respect my daughter's privacy. I'm just glad you two are together now, but I'm sure you can understand my reservations."

Shifting my weight nervously on my feet, I tuck my hands into the front pocket of my hoodie and nod. "I completely understand. Had I known about it, I would have been with her from the very start. We started things out as casual and I was honestly being stupid at the time. I was afraid Poppy would be a distraction from hockey and I wasn't ready to attempt to balance that so I pushed her away."

"I understand that, August. You're working hard to build a career that will support you and your family in the years to come. Trust me, my husband is a lawyer, so I understand the commitment your career demands. But, there is also a difference between being dedicated to your career and being married to it." She pauses for a moment, her eyes searching mine. "Your life is going to change with a baby. I need to know you understand that."

Swallowing hard over the knives in my throat, I nod, my hands growing clammy under her scrutinizing gaze. "I do. And I know Poppy and the baby will have to come first. I just need to figure out how to balance it all."

The sound of the doorbell echoes through the house, the sound dim as it reaches the closed-off den. I glance behind me, before looking back at Claudia who appears unaffected by the sound.

"I hope you do, because I don't want to see this baby grow up with its parents not together." She pauses for a second, her expression falling as a sad smile forms on her lips. "Poppy and her sister grew up being shuffled back and forth between two homes. Their father and I separated and he got remarried and ended up building a new family. When Evie died, Poppy and her father lost their relationship. It was devastating, but she managed to get through life without him dragging her down."

My heart is in my throat and I'm not sure how to process what she's telling me. Poppy never mentioned a sister before and given that Claudia just said that she passed away, I'm assuming that's why. She must sense the confusion and shock in my expression as her lips purse and her eyebrows draw together.

"Poppy didn't tell you about Evie, did she?"

I shake my head. "She mentioned you and your ex-husband not being together before, but that was it."

Claudia nods, her face solemn. "Poppy was there the night Evie died and I know it still pains her to talk about it. I just thought maybe she had talked to you about her. I'm sure she will when she's ready." She pauses for a moment, her eyes burning holes through mine. "I just need you to know that Poppy is strong and if she has to do this without you, she will."

Her words are like a punch to the gut, even though there is nothing menacing behind them. She's not saying it as a threat or a warning, just the cold hard truth. Poppy has endured enough heartache in life and still she pushes past it all. "She won't have to do it without me, Mrs. Vance--I mean, Claudia," I add as she cuts her eyes at me. "I want you to know that my intentions with your daughter come from a good place and I have nothing but her and the baby's best interests in mind."

"I hope so, August. Promises can be empty, but I hope yours are full." Her lips turn back into a smile and it isn't forced, it's genuine, even if she's still skeptical of me. I'll prove her wrong, though. Poppy and our child are the most important part of my life now. "That must be your parents. I need to be a good hostess, so why don't we go so you can introduce me to them?"

"Yes, of course," I smile, following after her as she pulls open the French doors and we step back into the hall. We enter the kitchen as Isla is introducing our parents to Poppy and her stepfather.

My mother's eyes meet mine from across the room and her face lights up as she strides over to me. "August," she says softly, wrapping her arms around me for a hug. "It's so nice to see you." She pauses, lowering her voice for just me to hear. "Poppy seems so lovely."

She steps away from me and I shake my father's hand as he steps up beside her. "Mom, Dad, this is Claudia, Poppy's mom." I turn toward her, motioning to my parents. "Claudia, my parents, Anna and Dennis."

They all smile at one another, hugging and shaking hands as they say their pleasantries. There's an immediate comfortableness that settles in the air as my mom and Claudia fall into an easy conversation and Benjamin and my father do the same. I walk deeper into the kitchen, joining Poppy, Isla, and Logan where they all finish the work that Claudia laid out for them.

"Hey, Claudia," Isla calls out to her as she grabs a bottle of wine and begins to pour some into glasses. "I think the food is done. Did you want us to start bringing it out to the table?"

Claudia glances over at the four of us, eagerly nodding. "That would be so sweet of you guys. I already have the table set, so we just need the food and we're good to go."

Isla and Logan each grab a different dish and I watch Poppy as she goes to grab one before I stop her. She looks up at me, her eyes meeting mine in confusion as I pull her hands away from the plate.

"Let me get it, baby," I murmur, my fingers stroking her arms. "You go sit down and save a seat for me next to you."

Poppy smiles up at me, nodding as she lets me direct her away from the counter. I watch her as she disappears into the dining room, unable to take my eyes off my girl. I'm so lost in her already, I'd be lying if I said I wasn't afraid. Developing attachments and getting close to someone like this is not my norm.

But I never had a choice with Poppy.

The choice was already made for us…

Just like the way we were made for each other.

CHAPTER TWENTY
POPPY

Dinner went better than I had expected. After meeting the Whitleys, I realized I was nervous for no reason. August's parents are just as warm and friendly as I hoped they would be. They accepted me and our situation with open arms and I couldn't have been happier with the way it went.

My mom and August's mother seemed to really hit it off. Isla made sure to corner the two of them so they could start planning the gender reveal party and a baby shower. Hearing them talk was overwhelming and Isla eventually made me leave the room, claiming it was top secret and I wasn't allowed to know what they were going to have planned.

I ended up in the den with August, his father, Logan, and Benjamin as they were all immersed in their talk of sports. After such a long drive and all of the excitement from dinner, I ended up drifting asleep on the couch. When I woke up, everyone had already left and August was carrying me to my bed.

Isla and Logan waited for him, since he was their ride home, and I could see how badly he didn't want to leave me. I struggled with the same feelings, because after spending the night with him before, one night together just didn't seem like it was enough. I was still so tired, though, so August made sure I was tucked in and comfortable before kissing my head and leaving with promises of calling me the next day.

As I roll out of bed now, I'm still tired, but have a long day of classes ahead of me. I'm getting closer and closer to graduation with each day and I can't let this slow me down now. Grabbing my phone from the nightstand, I see that I already have a message from August and a smile touches my lips.

AUGUST

> Good morning, beautiful. I know it's early, so I didn't want to wake you, but couldn't resist not at least leaving a message for you to find.

Rising to my feet, I shuffle across the room toward my bathroom, typing out a message to the boy who has his hands wrapped around my damn heart.

> **POPPY**
>
> What are you doing up so early? I have a break between my first two classes, so I will call you then if you aren't busy?

Setting my phone down on the counter in the bathroom, I use the toilet and wash my hands before brushing my teeth. August's message comes through, but I quickly run a hairbrush through my long strands before pulling it back in a ponytail.

> **AUGUST**
>
> We ended up having early practice. And I'm never too busy for you, baby. Call me whenever you can.

My heart soars and I'm riding on a cloud of ecstasy, the high of August coursing through my system. The effect he has on me scares me. I can't help but worry about the future and the what-ifs. It's a struggle, but I attempt to not focus on the thoughts that plague my mind. All I can do is take things one day at a time and hope for the best between August and I.

I just hope this doesn't eventually fall to pieces because dread fills me at the thought of the crash. And I'm afraid of the force of that fall.

After throwing on an oversized hoodie and a pair of sweatpants, I head over to campus and park my car as close as I can to the front. I'm tired as hell this morning, so having to walk too far across the parking lot seems like a daunting task. I have ten minutes until my first class begins, so I don't have to rush, but I like to get in and get my things organized before it starts.

As I'm walking into the building, I feel my phone begin to vibrate in the pocket of my sweatshirt. Veering off to the side, out of the way of other students, I stop along the wall and pull it out in a haste, checking the screen. My stomach rolls as I see that it's the doctor's office and I quickly answer it.

"Hello?"

"Hi, is this Poppy Williams?" The woman on the other end says, her voice warm and friendly. "I'm calling from The Woman's Place about scheduling your appointment for a 3D ultrasound with your anatomy scan."

"Yes!" I can barely contain the excitement from my voice as the butterflies violently flutter in my stomach. "This is Poppy. And I would love to go ahead and schedule that appointment."

"Would you be able to come in tomorrow, by any chance? We just had another patient have to reschedule their appointment, so we would be able to have both scans done back-to-back."

My heart crawls into my throat and tears instantly prick my eyes. "Yes, of course. I have classes all day, but I can make any time work."

The woman schedules my appointment for three in the afternoon tomorrow and I feel like a little kid on Christmas morning. As I end the call, I notice that I literally have two minutes left to get to my first class and it throws off my entire routine. But at this point, it doesn't even matter. We get to see our baby tomorrow.

And I need to tell August as soon as possible, because he is going to be ecstatic.

———

My first class feels like it's dragging. It could be because I'm more distracted than I should be and am barely paying attention to the lecture. After getting the call from the doctor's office, that's all that I can think about. That and August fucking Whitley.

Class wraps up and I'm one of the first people out the door, already pulling my phone out before I'm in the hall. Finding my messages, I tap on August's name and hit the Call button before bringing it up to my ear as it begins to ring.

He picks up on the second ring. "Hey, gorgeous. How was your first class?"

A stupid grin consumes my lips and I don't even bother attempting to hide it. "It was good. I'm just pretty tired this morning. How was practice?"

"It was good," he tells me, his voice matching mine with how tired he sounds. I can't even imagine having to get up early and skate the way they do. "I'm getting ready for class now and then have two this afternoon, thankfully."

"Well, that's good," I respond, stepping out of the way as I dodge another student who comes barreling down the hall as I make my way to my next class. "I'm glad you don't have a full day so you can relax."

"Speaking of relaxing," his voice is husky, the charm dripping from his words. "What are you doing after class? Come spend the night with me tonight?"

Chewing on the inside of my lip, I resist the urge to yell yes at him. Yesterday wasn't enough time with him and I'd much rather tell him in person about the appointment tomorrow. I want to see the look on his face when I tell him. "I would love to. When should I come over?"

"I get done with my last class around 4:30. Why don't you go home after your last one and pack a bag for the night and then just head over?" He pauses for a moment and I can hear the smile in his voice. "If I'm not home by then, Isla should be there. And you know I'll be on my way to you as soon as I can."

The smile doesn't leave my lips, the sound of his voice warming my soul in ways I never knew were possible. "I'll call Isla on my way to make sure she's home. I can't wait to see you."

"Me neither, baby. This day is going to drag ass now."

A soft laughter falls from my lips as I pause outside of the door to my next class. "It's only a few hours, babe. You'll see me sooner than you think."

August is silent for a moment. "Babe, huh? I think I like you calling me that."

"I gotta get to my next class, but I'll talk to you later, babe."

"Mmm," he murmurs into the phone. "Say it again, just one last time for me."

Laughter escapes me and I roll my eyes at him as I enter the classroom. "Bye, babe."

"Goddamn, I'm ready to see you." His voice is husky and I can hear the frustration in his words. "Fuck. Okay, I'll let you get to class. Later, beautiful."

Ending the call, I silence my phone and slide it back into the pocket of my hoodie as I find my seat. I sit down, not paying attention to anyone as I still hear August's voice in my head, and the damn grin is still on my face.

He's already worked his way under my skin, penetrating my soul. August has my heart and as much as it scares me to admit—I'm in deep, falling hard for him. There's nothing I can do to stop it from happening. All I can do is just fall and hope he's falling with me.

Even though our relationship is still relatively new, this has been growing between us for a long time. And now with a child, it just intensifies my feelings for him, especially seeing the effort he's been putting in. I never expected him to step up like he has and I'm so grateful for how caring and doting he has been.

Realization strikes me and it's a blow to my chest—hitting me directly in my heart.

I'm in love with August fucking Whitley.

CHAPTER TWENTY-ONE
AUGUST

The day literally fucking drags and I can't stop checking my phone. In college, they don't really have a strict policy about them because we're the ones that are here paying for our education. If we want to take that for granted, it's ultimately up to the students. But this is the first time I've actually been called out for having mine out, probably because of how goddamn excessive it's been.

I haven't necessarily been waiting for her to text me or call me or anything. Poppy is just as busy with her own classes. More than anything, I've been checking the time and counting down the minutes until I get to see my girl. I can't get enough of her and if I could have it my way, she would never leave my side.

She's gone above and beyond to make sure she's taking proper care of her health and keeping our baby healthy. In a way, it makes me feel useless. I'm watching it all happen from the outside. I just want to take care of her myself, to provide for her and make sure she's taken care of.

The first step I need to take is convince her to move in with me so I can take care of her.

We wouldn't have to live in the same apartment as Logan and Isla. They have their own shit going on and I'm sure they would like the privacy too. I think it's time for me to move out and get my own place. We don't have to live together forever and I'm in the process of starting my own family.

Poppy and our baby deserve the fucking world and that's exactly what I'm going to give them—nothing less.

As I pull up to our apartment building, I see Poppy's car already in the lot and my heart pounds erratically in my chest. I've been waiting all goddamn day for this moment, to walk in to see her. And knowing she's already here has my brain moving in fast forward. I barely put the car in park before I'm opening my door.

Pausing for a moment with one foot out the door, I kill the engine and leave my book bag in the car before climbing out. Shutting my door in a haste, I press the button to lock the door before striding directly into the building. The elevator doors are already open and I rush into it, slamming the button to shut it before pressing the one for our floor.

Usually my patience isn't running this thin, but the need to see her is driving me wild. The elevator stops at our floor and I'm sliding through the doors before they're fully open. As I reach our apartment, I turn the knob in a haste, hoping it's already unlocked, and much to my surprise, it is. I let myself in and the sound of laughter fills the air and I smile at the sound of my girl as the lilt of her laugh snakes its way around my eardrums.

Closing the door behind me softly, I walk through the kitchen, making sure to keep my footsteps light as I head into the dining room. The dining room opens up into the living room and I pause, watching the two of them on the couch laughing at some show they're watching. Poppy is curled up, covered with a blanket, looking like she belongs here.

Like a permanent fucking fixture in my life.

"What are the two of you cackling about?" I ask

loudly, walking into the living room as I catch them both by surprise. Poppy practically jumps out of her skin, her head turning to look at me, eyes wide. They soften as they meet mine and her smile matches my own.

Isla doesn't bother looking at me, rolling her eyes instead as she turns down the volume on the remote. "If you must know, we're watching the newest season of *Big Mouth*."

"You started it without me?" I question her, the sarcasm and pain in my words mixing together as I round the couch and sit down next to my girl.

"Oh, piss off, August," Isla scolds me, pausing the episode. "The entire season is on Netflix. Don't act like we watch every episode together."

Isla presses Play on it again as I laugh, wrapping an arm around Poppy's shoulders. She relaxes against me, curling her body toward mine as she lifts her head and kisses my cheek.

Sliding my hand under her chin, I turn her face to mine and gently press my lips to hers. "I missed you, baby," I murmur against her soft flesh. "So fucking much."

"I missed you too," she whispers, pulling away as her deep blue eyes search mine. "And I'll rewatch these episodes with you, if you really want to see them."

Her consideration and words send a warmth straight to my heart like an electrical current. A soft chuckle rumbles in my chest. "I've actually watched the entire season already. I just like fucking with Isla sometimes."

Isla jerks her head to the side, glaring at me as she launches a pillow at my head. Logan walks into the room, fresh from a shower as he eyes us all skeptically. A smile curls on his lips and he shakes his head as he disappears into the kitchen instead of engaging.

Lifting my arms, I shield Poppy and block it from hitting both of us. "Hey. You hit my baby momma with a pillow and you're gonna have hell to pay."

"Pfft, you know damn well that I wouldn't do anything to hurt Poppy or the baby," Isla snarls at me as she rises to her feet. "You, on the other hand... you're going to get it one of these days."

"Okay, children, let's stop fighting now," Logan calls out to us as he walks back into the room. "Isla, are you ready to go or are you going to spend the entire evening fighting with your brother?"

She sticks her tongue out like a child as she walks past me. Lifting my hand, I give her the middle finger, and she smacks the back of my head. Poppy laughs lightly, her eyes shining brightly at the interaction between us, but there's something else there. A shadow passes over her expression and a wave of pain washes over her blue irises.

The thought of her sister enters my mind and my heart instantly breaks for her. Poppy hasn't shared that part of herself with me yet, but after what her mother told me, I can't even imagine the pain she must feel on a daily basis. Isla might be a pain in my ass, but I can't imagine losing her. To have to continue living after her death. She's my sister and I can't fathom what life would be like without her in it.

"We'll be back later," Logan tells me, nodding as Isla grabs her coat and walks past him. "We're going to get dinner and figured we would give you guys some time alone."

"Thanks, bro." If there's one person I can count on to read the room, it's Logan. And he knows Poppy and I need the time alone, especially since we don't see each other every day like he and Isla do.

They both leave, their voices hushed as the door is pulled closed behind them. Turning in my seat, I face Poppy and brush a stray hair away from her face. Her eyes bounce back and forth between mine, the waves crashing in her oceanic irises.

"So, there's something I wanted to tell you earlier, but I wanted to wait until I saw you," she says softly as she bites back the smile that threatens to take over her lips. "The doctor's office called me this morning."

My stomach climbs into my throat and an unusual sense of dread fills me. The ghost of a smile on her lips is contradicting. Usually when people say that the doctor's office called them, it ends up being something bad. But she looks happy. I swallow back the anxious feeling and focus on her eyes as I wait for her to continue.

"You remember how we have the twenty-week anatomy scan and they said about doing a 3D ultrasound too? Well, they called to say they had an appointment available tomorrow at three o'clock."

And just like that, the dread is completely gone and I'm consumed by an overwhelming feeling I can't even put into words. It's a combination of joy and happiness—I'm fucking elated and overcome with so much emotion. Swallowing hard over the lump in my throat, I gently cup the sides of her face.

"A 3D one? Like where we can see the baby's face and everything?"

Poppy nods, the smile on her face so fucking infections, and she laughs lightly. "The anatomy scan is to make sure the baby is growing properly and we can find out what we're having. After that, we get the 3D one where we get to see the baby literally in 3D."

"Holy fucking shit," I whisper, my eyes wide as I stare back at her. "We really get to see our baby tomorrow? Oh my god. Wait. Do you want to know what we're having or do you want it to be a surprise?"

She laughs again, wrapping her arms around the back of my neck as my hands fall down to her hips. "I'm guessing you didn't hear your sister's plans?"

Shaking my head, I pull her closer until she's situated on top of my lap. "What does Isla have planned?" I murmur as I move my hands to her stomach, cupping the bump with my palms.

"We're not allowed to know what we're having. We're supposed to have the ultrasound tech write it on a piece of paper and put it in an envelope." She pauses for a moment as I lift my eyes back to hers. "The envelope goes to Isla and she's planning a gender reveal party for us."

A groan slips from my lips and my head falls back in an exaggerated manner. "Of course she wants to plan something so fucking extra. Can't we just find out and pretend we don't know?"

Poppy laughs again, pulling my head back up to face her. "Nope. It's going to be a surprise for us until the party."

Laughing, I shake my head at Poppy. "You have no idea what you've gotten us into by letting her handle it."

We both fall silent as Poppy stares directly through me, her eyes penetrating my soul. Swallowing hard over the lump in my throat, I get lost in the depths of her eyes, swimming in the waves that crash against the shore. Lifting her from my lap, I set her down on the couch, gently pushing her onto her back as I hover above her.

"What are you doing?" she croaks out, her voice nervous and an octave higher as she attempts to glance around.

Rocking back onto my shins, I stare down at her and slowly lift the bottom hem of her shirt up, stopping just before her breasts. I flatten my hands along her stomach, slowly stroking her swollen belly. Her eyes are on me, her throat bobbing as she swallows hard, and her eyes grow wet.

Leaning forward, I press my lips to her stomach, just above her belly button. "I still can't fucking believe it," I whisper against her skin as I kiss her again. "Our baby is growing inside of you right now." Lifting my head, my eyes find hers. "You're the most amazing person that I'll ever meet. And there's no one else that I would rather see carrying my child."

Tears begin to fall from Poppy's eyes and she swallows hard, her nose red as she stares up at me. Crawling over her, I wipe the droplets from the sides of her face, my eyes searching hers. "I love you, Poppy. And I'm not just saying that because you're pregnant. I tried to stop it from happening, but it was never an option. I'm so fucking in love with you."

Her eyes widen, rapidly searching mine. "Don't say that if you don't mean it, August."

Tilting my head to the side, a smile tugs on the corners of my lips. "I wouldn't be saying it to you if I didn't mean it. You're the only one and you will always be the only one for me."

Poppy's chest rises and falls with each shallow breath. I watch her face transform, her smile reaching her eyes as the tears begin to fall again. "I love you, August."

CHAPTER TWENTY-TWO
POPPY

August hovers above me, a smile on his lips as his eyes search mine. Tears stream down the sides of my face and he reaches for them, catching each one with the pads of his fingertips. He drags them down my cheeks, smearing the wetness across my face as his lips collide with mine.

Wrapping my arms around the back of his neck, he cups my cheeks as he consumes me, swallowing me whole. He keeps his weight off me, careful of my stomach as he steals the air from my lungs. His tongue slides along the seam of my lips, not waiting for me to part them as he slips inside.

The hormones and emotions have me instantly sliding my hands down his torso, grabbing at his shirt in a haste. His tongue tangles with mine, his lips bruising mine as he leaves his mark on me. I slide his shirt up to his shoulders before pushing him away from me.

August leans back, a sultry smirk playing on his lips as he pulls his shirt over his head. "Tell me what you want, baby," he murmurs, his face dropping down to mine.

"I want you to fuck me," I admit, my voice catching in my throat as I attempt to glance around the room. "Can we go to your bedroom, though? What if Logan and your sister get back?"

August shakes his head, chuckling lightly. "Nope. They won't be back for a while. And I'm fucking you right here, right now."

My lips part as I attempt to argue with him, but he silences me as his mouth collides with mine again. Putting my common sense to the side, I let the lust take the driver's seat and it's suddenly a rush to the top of the cliff we're climbing together. My hands find the waistband of his joggers and I'm struggling to push them down as he's pushing my shirt up higher.

He sits up, pulling me with him as he effortlessly slides my shirt over my head and tosses it onto the floor. Reaching around my back, he unclasps my bra and peels it away from my body. My breasts ache with need, my nipples hardening under his gaze as he looks at me like I'm his last fucking meal.

Gently pushing my back against the couch, he reaches for my sweatpants and swiftly pulls them down my thighs, dragging my panties down with them. In an instant, they're gone and discarded on the floor as he brings his face down to my pussy.

His breath is warm against me and I squirm as he licks me, wetting me with his tongue. My hands find his hair and I jerk him away, pulling him back up to me.

"As fucking amazing as your tongue feels, I want your cock right now."

August chuckles lightly, a sinister look in his eyes as they search mine. "Greedy, are we?"

"Take off your pants," I order him, as I attempt to lean forward and strip them from his body myself.

He plants his hand against my chest, pushing me back down to the couch as he shakes his head at me. "Bossy, too," he murmurs as he rises from the couch. Sliding his fingers under the waistband of his joggers, I watch as he pushes them down his toned thighs, taking his boxers with him. As he stands back upright, his cock is hard as a rock. August climbs back over me, a smirk playing on his lips. "As much as I like you being bossy, I'm the one who's in control, beautiful."

My pussy is wet and pulsating with need. August settles between my legs, spreading my thighs apart as he presses his cock against my center. His movements are slow as he moves his hips forward, slowly sliding inside me. A moan falls from my lips and his mouth collides with mine as he fills me to the brim.

August doesn't stop until the entire length of his cock is inside me, filling me deeply as his balls touch me. A moan slips from my lips again and he swallows the sounds as his tongue swirls with mine. My hands find his back, my nails digging into his flesh as he slides a hand around the back of my neck and plants the other on the couch beside my head.

Pulling back his hips, he stops with just the tip inside before easing back into me. He continues his slow assault, taking his time as he fucks me slowly. Lifting my hips, I meet him stroke for stroke, taking his thick girth as he rubs the inside of my pussy.

"I can't wait any longer, baby," he murmurs against my lips, nipping at my bottom one. "I've waited all fucking day to see you. I'm not done with you after this, but I'm gonna fuck you. Hard."

The sound of his voice vibrates through my body and a warmth spreads across my stomach, the ecstasy already building. His cock pulsates inside me, his balls tight against my ass. His release is so close and I can't fault him for that. He wanted to please me first, but I wanted this. I wanted to feel him this close and inside me.

Right now, my pleasure doesn't even matter to me, even though this feels so fucking good. I want him to feel good and take what he wants and needs from me.

"Fuck me, babe," I breathe against his mouth. "I want you to fuck me hard until you're filling me with your cum."

He pulls back slightly, his eyes searching mine with a sudden look of concern. "If it hurts, promise me you'll tell me and I'll stop."

"I promise," I assure him, wrapping my legs around his waist. Pulling him back to me, he thrusts inside, this time harder. "Now, stop talking and fuck me like you promised."

August follows my order, his gaze heated as he stares down at me and fucks me like his life depends on it. Planting both hands beside my head, he pistons his hips, slamming harder into me with each thrust. The warmth spreads through my body, my orgasm coming on quickly as August drives us closer and closer to the edge.

One last thrust and he sends us soaring over the cliff, deeper and deeper into the abyss of ecstasy. My name falls from his lips like a prayer. He fills me with his cum as my pussy clenches around him, both of our orgasms tearing through our bodies.

August hovers above me as we both ride the lasting waves of our high, my pussy feeling his absence as he slowly eases out of me. Leaning forward, he presses his lips to my forehead. "I love you, baby." He rises to his feet, sliding his arms under the back of my head and the backs of my knees as he lifts me from the couch. "Let me draw you a bath and take care of you."

I stare into his eyes as he carries me into the bathroom, my heart swelling as it's about to burst from my chest. I've never felt anything like this before and the way he cares is enough to make me melt into a puddle at his feet.

I'm so hopelessly in love with him.

When I leave for class the next morning, I make sure not to disturb August before disappearing from his apartment. We were both exhausted when we finally fell asleep, after having quite the night together. After he fucked me in the living room, we took it back to his bedroom where he locked us away, only taking a break to feed me dinner because I was starving.

Practices have been getting longer and more grueling for him since they have their tournament coming up soon. It's taking a lot out of him and I don't know how he manages to stay focused on his schoolwork. I had heard through the grapevine that schools will actually fabricate people's scores if it's more important having them as a star on a sports team.

I haven't asked August about that because I don't think it's true with him. Sure, it probably happens in some places, but I've seen him study. He's just as dedicated to that as he is to hockey. Everyone needs to have some type of a fallback plan, although I don't think he will realistically need it.

When I left him, he looked so peaceful, too innocent to bother. I was careful and quiet when I slipped out of his room, his soft snores coming from where his head was buried in the pillows. As badly as I wanted to stay with him, I can't lose focus on my end goal here, even if August is involved in everything now.

I refuse to rely on someone else because when it comes down to it, the only person that I can really depend on is myself.

August texts me about mid-morning, telling me he forgot to charge his phone overnight and it might die, but he would see me this afternoon at the appointment. I sent him a text back, wishing him a good day, and he sent me a winking emoji back.

The day felt like it took forever to be over, but before I knew it, it was time to head to my appointment. I've been counting down the minutes for this appointment, to finally get to see our baby in 3D. When I pull into the parking lot, I don't see August's car, so I send him a text letting him know where I am.

But now that I'm sitting in the waiting room alone, I'm beginning to question where he is. I checked in almost ten minutes ago and there's still no sign of him. The nurse had already come out once for me and I asked her if she could give me a few minutes since I was waiting for my boyfriend to get here. Pulling my phone from the pocket of my coat, I check and see that my message was delivered but wasn't received.

In a haste, I tap on his name in an attempt to call him. My stomach falls, a wave of dread washing over me as it goes directly to voicemail. The nurse comes out for a second time, her eyes finding mine as a look of sympathy fills them.

"Poppy, I'm so sorry, but we have to start your appointment now or else you're going to have to reschedule." Her voice is soft and she offers a sympathetic smile. "I'm sorry he isn't here, but we have other appointments scheduled after yours."

Emotion wells in my throat, lodging in there like a fucking dam. I attempt to swallow it back, but I'm unable to as tears prick the corners of my eyes. "It's fine," I choke out, coughing to cover up the way my voice cracks. "We can get started without him."

The nurse nods in understanding, but I don't miss the way that she still stares at me with pity in her eyes. I follow behind her, my footsteps heavy and slow as the pit of my stomach rolls. It feels like my heart was completely ripped out of my chest. He promised me he would be here, so where the hell is he?

Anger boils inside me, my jaw clenching at the thought of him, but I can't cling to the feeling. The pain is stronger and my heart cracks, slowly falling into pieces inside its cage like a dead flower petal.

He told me his phone was going to die, but it's not like he wouldn't have had access to a charger somewhere.

The least he could have done was called and told me he wasn't going to make it, instead of making me look like a fucking fool waiting for him.

The nurse checks my weight and my blood pressure before the doctor comes in and does an exam. It's such a struggle to try and focus on all of it when I can't help but get lost in the thought of August and his deception. After the exam is over, the nurse leads me back to the ultrasound room, where the tech takes me in and instructs me to go to the bathroom and get on the table afterward.

She leaves the room to give me privacy and I slip into the bathroom, splashing cool water on my face in an attempt to bring me back to reality. I hastily wipe at the lingering tears and get myself together before heading back out into the room. As I settle on the table and cover myself up with a blanket, she knocks on the door and comes back inside.

"Are we finding out what you're having today?" she asks as she squeezes some warm lube on my stomach and begins to move the probe across it as she stares at the TV screen on the wall.

Swallowing hard over the lump in my throat, I

stare at the screen, watching as she moves past different blurs that I can't tell what it actually is. "Actually, are you able to write it on a piece of paper and put it in an envelope so I can't see it?"

As I glance over at her, her face lights up, a bright smile forming on her lips. "Of course. I love gender reveals. That's so fun and exciting!"

"Yeah." I force a smile and a soft laugh that barely sounds like it's even a real sound. "It should be interesting."

The ultrasound tech falls silent as the awkwardness fills the room from my terse attitude. I can't help it, but it's so hard to swallow back the pain and the disappointment that is fucking with my heart and my head right now.

"So, I'm just checking over everything to make sure your organs look good and then we will move on to the baby."

Nodding, I stare at the screen absentmindedly, attempting to focus on the feeling of the probe gliding across my stomach with the lube. I can't tell what we're looking at still and the ultrasound tech points out specific things as she presses buttons on her machine, but I'm not fully paying attention.

I can't help but wish August would come bursting through the door right now, but I know that won't happen. This isn't a fantasy or a movie. Things in real life don't happen like that. Regardless of what I want to happen—August isn't showing up.

"Okay, let's check out the baby," the tech says, smiling at me as she begins to move the probe again and the image pops up on the screen.

My breath catches in my throat as I stare at our baby as it moves inside my stomach. It's easy to make out the shape of its head and its spine. Its lips and nose. The tech explains everything as she moves the probe around, smiling as she tells me that everything looks exactly how it should be.

"Let me switch some things around and we'll begin the 3D ultrasound," she says as she hands me a strip of paper that has all of the pictures she just took. "Here's some for your memories and to share with whoever you'd like. I'll have the envelope with the sex when we're done here."

My heart pounds erratically in my chest, my throat constricting as I stare at the strip of pictures in my hand. August only got to hear the baby's heartbeat. He has yet to see a real ultrasound like this and he isn't fucking here for it. I still can't believe it—after everything, I didn't expect him to let me down like this. He knew how important this appointment was.

The tech comes back to me with a different machine as she applies more lube and begins to move the probe over my stomach. Staring at the screen, my breath catches as a perfectly little symmetrical face appears in front of me.

"There's your little one," the tech says, the smile audible in her voice. "You got lucky. Sometimes they aren't this cooperative and it's hard to see their faces. I guess your baby wanted Mama to see their face."

Tears instantly spring to my eyes before they begin to spill down my cheeks. As I stare at the screen, reality slaps me directly across the face and I can feel the blow in my chest. My heart constricts as it breaks into a million pieces. This is the only thing that matters—this tiny human I'm growing inside my stomach.

Nothing else.

August not showing up showed his true colors. His priorities are completely fucked up and if he can't put this child before everything, then there is no way this will ever work between us. I refuse to rely on him, but if he isn't going to show up for the important things in our life, then there is no future for the two of us.

My heart is in my throat as I stare at the little

face, watching as they part their plump lips on the screen. This baby needs me more than anything... and I can't be worrying about August when I need to focus on what really matters.

If this appointment wasn't enough for him to show up, who's to say what is actually important to him?

I knew when I got involved with him that hockey would always come first...

I just didn't think it would come before his own child.

CHAPTER TWENTY-THREE
AUGUST

Fucking practice kicked my ass and I'm ready to charge my phone, call my girl and go to sleep. After last night with her, I did not get enough sleep and literally made my way through the day like a damn zombie. By the time the afternoon rolled around, my phone had already died and we had an emergency team meeting, which then promptly turned into a practice.

Poppy had a doctor's appointment today and I feel like a complete piece of shit for missing it. There's no way I would have been able to leave practice without completely fucking myself, though. Coach would have taken away playing time from me and that's too important to lose right now.

From what I read online, she's only five months

into the pregnancy, so there will be other ultrasounds and appointments that I will be able to go to. I know I should have found a way to call Poppy, but I literally didn't have a chance to.

"You good, bro?" Logan asks as we drive closer to our apartment. "You look like you could throw up or something."

"I missed Poppy's appointment today. And my phone died so I couldn't even call her to tell her that I wasn't going to make it." I pause for a moment, clenching my jaw as I stare out the window as rain begins to fall against the glass. "She's going to be fucking pissed."

Logan is silent for a moment, navigating through the rain. "If you just explain it to her, you don't think she will understand?"

As we pull into the parking lot of our apartment building, I see Poppy's car sitting in one of the spots in the front row. Swallowing hard over the lump in my throat, I glance at Logan as he puts the car in park. "I guess we're about to find out."

The rain starts falling harder and I pull my hood up over my head as Logan pops the trunk. We grab our stuff from it and he shuts the door as we begin to walk toward the apartment building. Both of us are silent, me lost in my own thoughts and Logan just being silent because, what the fuck could he possibly say?

It feels like an eternity as we get onto the elevator and take it to our floor. I swear, by the time that we get out, I'm surprised we're still in the same lifetime. The hallway is empty and I let out an exasperated sigh, thankful that Poppy isn't out here waiting for me.

I don't know which is worse... her waiting in the hall or knowing that she's in there with my sister. I don't even want to think about the shit she's going to give me after she watches this blow up. She's grown protective over Poppy, and I'm thankful for it, don't get me wrong. But the last thing I need is her on my shit too.

"Want me to go in first?" Logan asks me, his voice wary as he reaches for the doorknob.

Meeting his blue eyes, I shrug, my grip tightening on the stick in my hand. "It doesn't matter. Let's just go in, okay?"

Logan nods, slowly turning the knob as he pushes open the door. The apartment is silent as we walk in and for a moment, I'm confused. We don't hear the sounds of Isla's or Poppy's voices or the TV playing. Surely, they're not sitting here in silence. The entire thing feels off and I can feel the heaviness hanging in the air as I push the door shut behind me.

I set my bag near the closet door, propping my stick up next to Logan's as I watch him walk through the kitchen. The sound of hushed voices come through the dining room and I pause for a moment, collecting myself before I head in the direction of them.

As I walk through the door that leads into the dining room, I see Isla and Poppy sitting at the table, both of them staring directly at me. Logan stands over near the living room and he gives me a sympathetic smile as I meet his gaze before he disappears down the hall with his hockey bag behind him.

"I should be going," Poppy tells Isla, her voice cracking as she pushes back her chair and rises from her seat. "Thank you again for handling the gender reveal party."

"Of course," my sister tells her, her smile not quite reaching her eyes as the awkwardness hangs heavily in the air. "I'll make sure no one else knows what it says inside here," she says, lifting the envelope up.

Isla rises from her chair, her eyes narrowing as she meets my gaze. She walks directly toward me, stopping as her toes reach mine. She's more than a foot shorter than me, so she has to tilt her head back to look up at me, but that doesn't take away from the harsh fucking look written across her face.

"You better make this fucking right, August," she mumbles, attempting to keep her voice low, but I don't miss the threat lingering in her words. "You really fucked up this time."

Shaking her head at me in disappointment, she swiftly spins on her heel and strides over to Poppy. I watch, shifting my weight awkwardly as my sister pulls my girlfriend in for a hug and whispers something to her before they part. Isla glances at me once more over her shoulder, her eyes colder than the ice that we skate on. She looks back at Poppy, smiling once more before she disappears down the hall to her and Logan's room.

My eyes find Poppy, desperately searching her face, but she avoids my gaze, her eyes cast at the floor as she wrings her hands in front of her. She doesn't move for a moment, so I take my chance and move closer to her, reaching out for her.

"Poppy, please, just let me explain," I plead, my voice cracking as she flinches, moving away from me as I get closer to her. It's a blow directly to the chest and my breath catches.

She lifts her gaze to mine, her blue eyes frigid

and glazed over as the tears well in the corners of them. "Why couldn't you have the decency to call me and tell me you weren't going to make it? Do you know how goddamn stupid I looked, asking the nurse to just wait ten more minutes in case you showed up?"

"I'm sorry, baby," I murmur, not fully trusting my voice as emotion thickens my throat. "Fuck. I'm so sorry. I should have called, but my phone died and I didn't have a chance to charge it."

"No," she growls, her voice hard. "You don't get to stand here and apologize and make excuses, August. That's not how this works. You knew how important this appointment was and you promised me you would be there. How the hell am I supposed to put any weight on anything you say?"

Her words slice through my heart, severing my rib cage as the blade reaches the vital organ inside. "Fuck, Poppy. Our coach called an emergency meeting and then it was an unplanned practice. I couldn't just leave or I would end up getting playing time cut from me as a punishment."

Poppy snorts, her eyebrows drawn together as her face contorts. "That's what this always comes down to, isn't it? Fucking hockey," she sneers, shaking her head in disbelief. "If you can't make our baby a priority, how the fuck is this ever going to work between us? I need a partner who is going to be there for me—one who is going to be present and show up when they're fucking supposed to."

I stare back at her, her words completely rocking me to my core. My lips part slightly, but I have no legitimate response. She's so fucking right and there's nothing I can do to take it back. At that moment, it seemed like I didn't have a choice. Hockey was the only one that made sense at the time because I didn't realize how important this was to her.

But as I stand here and watch the waves of pain crash against the shores in her irises, I can't help but feel an overwhelming amount of guilt. Not only that, but the disappointment in myself for letting her down. I should have showed up, but I didn't. And I don't know what the hell to do about it.

"Poppy, please," I plead with her, fighting the urge to drop down on my knees in front of her. "I'm so goddamn sorry. Let me make this right, let me show you that you and the baby are the most important things to me."

Poppy stares back at me, the tears falling from her eyes without any inhibition. "It's too late for that, August. You made your choice and I can't even stand to look at you right now."

"Baby, don't do this…"

Poppy takes a step toward me, grabbing two strips of paper from the table and shoving them against my chest. "Here, August. This is what you missed today. Have a good fucking night."

Grabbing for the papers, I catch them before they fall to the floor as she brushes past me. Spinning on my heel, I turn around as I watch her walk away from me. "Poppy, please. Just give me a chance."

As she reaches the door, she turns to look at me one last time. The anger has dissipated from her expression and there's nothing but hurt left in its place. "I'm sorry, August…"

Her voice trails off, her words hanging heavily in the thickness of the air as she disappears through the door. I could go after her, but I'm cemented in place as my gaze falls down to the strips of paper in my hands. My eyes scan them, trailing over the pictures of our baby in black and white before I flip to the 3D pictures.

Emotion wells in my throat, the lump forming, and I can't swallow it down as a sob falls from my lips. Our baby—our perfect little combination of the best parts of us. I can't tear my eyes away from the pictures, as I memorize the delicate features of our little one that is growing inside Poppy's stomach.

My heart cracks and I fall to my knees on the floor as realization sets in.

I really fucked up this time...

And I don't know whether Poppy is ever going to forgive me for this.

CHAPTER TWENTY-FOUR
POPPY

Seeing August didn't help with the anger or the pain that completely floods me. It's pouring as I drive back home and I can't stop the tears that blur my vision. The rain begins to fall harder, the droplets pelting on the windshield as I pull over on the side of the road and succumb to the aching in my chest. My soul hurts gravely and I can't fight the sobs as they tear through my body.

I know it wasn't entirely August's fault, but I can't help but feel like he let me down too. This was his opportunity to prove himself and he failed to come through. I refuse to be the one that comes between him and his dreams, but I won't let him be the reason that mine don't come true too.

We were destined for heartbreak from the

moment we met. And knowing there's a baby involved makes it hurt that much more.

It was foolish of me to think this would ever actually work out. I knew from the start it was a gamble and a risk, being with someone who was so immersed in their own life. Stupid me for thinking there was any space in his life for me. Maybe my expectations were too high. I always knew he wouldn't be able to fully commit, but there was a part of me that hoped he would make a conscious effort to put us first.

I was wrong... so goddamn wrong.

The tears slowly begin to subside and I hastily wipe them away from my face before I pull my car back onto the road and head back home. My phone rings from the cupholder beside me, but I don't bother looking at it, as I already know it's him. Funny, now he can call me when he knows that everything between us is on the line.

Reaching for my phone, I pick it up and silence it before dropping it back into the cupholder. My soul hurts and my mind is blank as I drive home, not realizing how close I am until I'm pulling into the driveway. As I turn off my car, I inhale deeply before heading back into the rain and make my way into the house.

It's dark and silent inside and I don't bother looking for my mother. I walk right past the bathroom, skipping the bath that would normally calm me. Instead, I lock myself in my room, stripping out of my wet clothes before slipping into my bed.

My phone begins to light up as message after message from August comes through. I try to ignore it, but it continues as he starts to call me too. The tears prick the corners of my eyes again and I can't take the painful reminder of him, even though he invades every inch of my mind. Reaching over, I grab my phone from where I set it on the nightstand and power it off.

Burying my head in the pillow, I pull the blankets up over my head, cocooning myself in the warmth of my bed as I let my sadness pull me back under. The tears don't stop falling and I don't bother fighting it as I succumb to the pain and effectively cry myself to sleep.

The next morning, I wake up feeling like total shit. My eyes feel swollen from crying, and my chest aches from the hole inside my heart. With my phone being turned off, I didn't have my alarm, so I missed my first few classes of the morning. I should care, but there's a part of me that really doesn't.

Grabbing my phone, I don't bother turning it on as I tuck it into the pocket of my bag and head downstairs. My mom is sitting in the kitchen and I'm surprised she's here and not at work.

"What are you doing home?" I ask her, as I walk to the fridge and grab a bottle of water.

"I could ask you the same thing," she retorts, her eyes filled with worry as they search mine and she takes a sip of her coffee. "I noticed you were still home, so I wanted to make sure you were okay. I didn't want to wake you, though, when I saw you were still sleeping."

I nod, grabbing a banana from the counter. "I'm okay, I just had a rough night and overslept this morning. I'll email my professors and see if they can email me the stuff I missed so I can stay on track."

My mother nods, but I can see in her eyes that she's hanging onto one key point from what I just rambled to her. "Why did you have a rough night? Did something happen?"

A sigh slips from my lips and I shrug. "I had my 3D ultrasound appointment yesterday." I pause for a moment, mentally kicking myself for leaving the pictures with August because I wanted to show them to her. "August didn't show up for it."

"Did you talk to him?"

I nod, shifting my weight as I stand in the center of the kitchen. "I did. And I don't think he's reliable. I need someone I can count on and he proved that hockey is more important. I refuse to make him choose between me or what he's worked so hard for his entire life."

My mother purses her lips, a look of sympathy in her eyes. "Does he know this is how you feel?"

"I don't know," I tell her honestly as I attempt to replay the night in my head, but it hurts too much to think about. "I didn't come out and end things with him, but I've thought about it all night and I think it's for the best."

"I just don't want you to make any rash decisions, but if you feel like this is what has to happen, you know I support whatever choice you make."

I smile at her, but it doesn't reach my eyes. "Thanks, Mom. I should probably go, though, so I can try and get to my afternoon classes."

"Are you sure you don't want to just take the day off? It's okay to not be okay sometimes, Poppy." She pauses for a moment, a wave of pain washing over her eyes. My mind drifts to the same place hers does... Evie. The one person who tried to hold it all together until she couldn't. Until the weight of the world began to drag her down...

My eyes grow misty as I stare back at my mother. "I really wish she were here sometimes. I know she had her struggles, but she could have overcome them. She was always stronger than she gave herself credit for."

"I wish she was here too, sweetheart." My mother's voice cracks as tears fill her eyes. "She had so much life in her, I just wish she could have seen the light that was hiding in her darkness. You know, we tried to get her help, but I don't think we did enough."

I stare back at my mother, my heart breaking for her. Instinctively, I place my hand over my stomach and I can't bear the thought of how she must feel after losing her own child. "You did everything you could for her. Evie was spiraling and I don't think anything would have helped unless she wanted the help. If I would have stopped her from diving in that night, she would have still had a chance, though."

My mother rises to her feet, walking toward me as a sob tears through my body. She wraps her arms around me, pulling me into her warmth as she holds me, and I cry against her shoulder. "Shhh," she murmurs, stroking my hair. "It wasn't your fault, honey. You have to stop blaming yourself for it. Focusing on the what-ifs will never bring her back. It was Evie's choice, not yours, and you are not to blame for what happened."

Collecting myself, I pull away from her, taking a step back as I hastily wipe the tears from my eyes. "I know, but sometimes the guilt gets the best of me. I'm trying."

"That's all we can do, Poppy. We all try our best and make the most out of our lives." She pauses, smiling at me with a look of pride in her eyes. "You have so much ahead of you, please don't let the past get in the way of that."

"I love you, Mom," I tell her as I walk past her, heading toward the front door.

"Love you always," she calls out after me. I slip outside, feeling the warmth of the sun on my black coat, which is a contrast to the dark cloud that hangs over my head. As I get into my car, thoughts of August plague my mind again. I know I need to talk to him and face him, I just don't think I'm ready to yet.

I'm not ready for this to be over, but I know it's what I have to do.

My afternoon classes go by a lot faster than I planned. It's enough to keep me distracted from my thoughts of August and I'm able to get all of the notes from my professors from this morning. Pulling out my phone, I power it on and quickly ignore everything from August before sending my mother a message. I let her know I'm going to order food and spend the evening in the library catching up on my missed work.

She tells me to check in with her when I get home and I send her a message back, letting her know that I will, before I power my phone off again. I can't bring myself to look at any of August's texts yet and I don't want to chance having him reach out again.

The library is relatively empty when I get there after my last class. Finding an empty table, I settle in with my things, setting up my laptop before putting in my AirPods. Pulling my books and notes from my bag, I spread them across the wooden surface and allow it to consume my focus as I lose myself in my work.

I don't know how much time passes, but I'm completely immersed in my classwork, working my ass off to get caught back up. I can't afford to fall behind now. My grades have been exceptional and I don't want my GPA to drop because of a small hiccup in life.

As I'm reading over something on my laptop, I hear the librarian speaking to someone in a flustered voice. Pulling out my one AirPod, I listen in on the conversation, not turning around to make it obvious since her desk is behind me.

"I'm sorry, but you're not a student here," she says, the emphasis thick in her voice. She's entirely frustrated and sounds like she's at her wit's end. "I can't allow you to come into the library if you don't attend school here."

"Look, I promise that I will be quick. There's someone I need to see in here and I will leave as soon as I talk to her."

His voice sends a shiver down my spine and I freeze in my seat. The sound of his husky tone snakes its way around my eardrums, wedging itself in my soul. August fucking Whitley.

Pulling out my other AirPod, I set it down on the table and let out a ragged breath as I slide out of my seat. Rising to my feet, I slowly turn around and see him leaning against her desk, still arguing with her.

My heart pounds erratically in my chest, my

palms clammy as I walk on shaky legs toward the two of them. The librarian lifts her eyes to me, her face flush and flustered. "I'm so sorry, Mrs. Edwards," I begin, my voice apologetic as I silently plead with my eyes. "You'll have to excuse him. He's here to see me."

"See," August throws his hands up as an exasperated sigh slips from his lips. "I told you I was here to see someone."

Mrs. Edwards looks between the two of us, narrowing her eyes. "Please take this out into the hall. There are other students trying to study here and you've already caused enough disruption," she snaps at August.

August nods and I offer her an apologetic smile, before I grab his hand and drag him out into the hall. As we step out into the space, I close the library doors behind us and turn to him, crossing my arms over my chest.

"What are you doing here, August?"

His eyes are wild and he looks like he hasn't slept at all. His clothes are wrinkled and disheveled, his hair a tousled mess on top of his head. "You haven't been answering any of my texts or calls. You turned off your phone. I'm going crazy, baby. I needed to see you and talk to you."

My heart rattles inside its cage, threatening to break through my ribs as I stare at him. "Did it ever occur to you that I turned off my phone because I didn't want to talk to you or see you right now?"

"I know, I know," he says, running a frustrated hand through his hair. "I just needed to see you. I need you to understand that I didn't mean to miss the appointment yesterday. Seriously, it's been tearing me up inside and I just want to make it up to you."

His words break my heart, but I know staying with him will only shatter it. "It's not something you can make up for, August. That's the thing... I've been thinking about it all night and I know what has to be done."

He narrows his eyes at me, his face scrunching up in distaste. "What does that mean?"

I swallow hard over the lump lodged in my throat. "We can't be together. I'm not saying you can't be involved in the baby's life, because I want you to be a part of it. But this isn't going to work with us."

He recoils, looking at me like I just slapped him across the face. "Don't do this, baby. Please... just give me a chance to show you I can be what you need. That you're more important to me than anything."

My heart continues to break, the shards falling to the floor around my feet as I watch his face crumble. "I'm sorry, August. I won't make you choose between hockey and me. You've worked too hard to give that up. I know how important it is to you and I can't be the reason you throw it all away. You're destined for greatness, but we're not."

"Poppy..." His voice cracks, trailing off as tears rapidly fill his eyes. "I'm fucking begging you not to do this."

"I love you, August... but sometimes love just isn't enough."

His lips part slightly, but no words come out as he stares at me in utter shock. I can't bear to look at him anymore as my resolve is slowly waning, watching his heart break in his chest. Spinning on my heel, I quickly put as much distance as I can between us, disappearing back into the library.

My heart waits for him to come after me, but he doesn't.

He doesn't come running for me... and I know this is really it.

Our relationship is officially over.

CHAPTER TWENTY-FIVE
AUGUST

Standing in the hallway, my eyes are glued to the doors of the library Poppy disappeared through. I don't know what I was thinking, coming here, but I didn't anticipate it turning out this way. I should do something, but what can I possibly do? Resisting the urge to march back into the library and confront her again, I turn on my heel and slowly make my way back out of the building.

I wasn't expecting Poppy to say that everything would be okay. I fucked up by not showing up and coming through for her. It's all my fault and there's nothing I can do about it now. Poppy needs some space and maybe that will help to change her mind.

Either way, I can't just sit around and do nothing about this. I'll walk away and give her some time, but this is far from over. Contrary to what Poppy thinks, I'll never be done with her and I'm not going to let something like this get in the way of my end goal.

When I get back home, Isla and Logan are sitting at the dining room table, eating dinner. There's a plate sitting out for me, but right now my appetite is nonexistent. Both of them fall silent when I enter the room, their questioning eyes on me as I take my seat and push the empty plate toward the center of the table.

"How did it go?" Logan is the first to question me as Isla gives me a death stare from across the table. When it comes to the two of them, Logan is always the lesser evil to deal with. When it comes down to it, he's my best friend and he's more likely to take my side. He might still shoot me straight and tell me when I'm being an idiot, but when it comes to matters of the heart, he seems to be more understanding.

My sister, on the other hand... she looks at me like she wants to drive the fork in her hand into my eye sockets.

"Not well," I admit, grabbing the glass of water in front of me as I take a sip. "Poppy made it pretty clear that this is over."

Isla's eyebrows draw together as she glares at me, her top lip curling in disgust. "And that's it? You're seriously just going to accept that and move on instead of trying to make things better?"

Narrowing my eyes at her, I set my glass down in a rush, the liquid sloshing around in the cup. "Did I say that? Of course I'm not giving up on her. Jesus, Isla. This all just happened—what do you want me to do? Force her to be with me?"

"No," she says slowly, her tone softer as her expression falls. "She would be a fool to be with you when your priorities are all fucked up, and Poppy doesn't strike me as an idiot."

"How are my priorities fucked up? Because I missed an appointment due to a practice I had no control over?"

Logan doesn't say a word and he casts his gaze down to his plate of food before shoveling another forkful in his mouth. And this is when my best friend taps out. When his girlfriend—my sister—has her fangs pointed at my throat, Logan always backs down. He only intervenes if Isla is really out of line, so maybe she isn't in this moment.

"Look, I get it because I grew up in a household where our lives revolved around hockey," Isla starts, pausing for a moment as she sets her fork down on the table. "Poppy is new to all of this and doesn't understand the sacrifices that families have to make when someone is so immersed in this world. From the way she's seeing things right now, I'm sure it might look like hockey is more important than her and the baby."

I stare back at her, her words soaking in, but I can't help but jump straight to the defensive. "But that's not the case. Yeah, hockey has always been my life and my main priority because of making it to the NHL. Things have changed since Poppy and the baby, but I can't give up hockey entirely."

I don't know what the hell to even do right now…

"You don't have to give it up… you just have to find some kind of balance." Isla glances at Logan, who offers no advice as he shoves more food in his mouth. "Poppy is going to have to make sacrifices, but so are you. The least you could do is charge your goddamn phone and maybe reach out to her if plans change. I'm sure if you would have done that in the first place, this wouldn't even be an issue like this."

Isla is right. Poppy said as much, but I don't know how I can change what has already happened. I know I should have reached out to her, but I'll be honest, I lost track of time, and fuck—my sister is right. I didn't make it a priority like I should have.

The appointment might have been one of the most important ones and I wasn't there for it. At the time, it wasn't in the forefront of my mind that it was that important. After seeing Poppy's face and the way she reacted, I now know I was wrong. So fucking wrong.

I can understand her reservations and why she wouldn't want to be involved with me. Poppy was so damn unselfish, refusing to make me choose between her and hockey, and I am so grateful for that. That might have been the hardest decision I would have ever had to make.

The thought never crossed my mind in the past because hockey was always the most important thing. I kept things superficial and at face value for that main purpose. Attachments were never formed because I didn't want it to ruin my dreams and goals. If you would have asked me six months ago, hockey would have always been my first priority, no hesitation.

I can't confidently say that now. Would I hate to make that choice? Sure. But if I had to, I would and I now can see what is more important. When it comes down to it. I would choose Poppy. I will always choose her.

"How can I make this better?" I ask the two of them, looking to Logan for some kind of guidance. He has more experience with relationships and making them work than I do. "I need her to know she comes first over everything."

Logan shrugs. "Grovel, bro. There's literally nothing else you can do but beg for her forgiveness."

"Words aren't everything," Isla interjects, as she finishes the food on her plate. "You have to show her too. You could literally tell her whatever you wanted to, but when it comes down to it at the end of the day, your actions are what are going to be the deciding factor for changing her mind."

I look back and forth between the two of them. "How the hell am I supposed to show her? Give up hockey?"

"Absolutely not," Logan tells me without hesitation, earning a sideways glance from Isla. He doesn't miss it and turns to look at her. "After the years of fucking work your brother has put in, you really think he should give up hockey?"

Isla lifts an eyebrow at him. "I didn't say that, I just found it interesting how you didn't hesitate at all." She pauses for a moment, rolling her eyes. "If there is anyone who is a faithful, blind supporter of their significant other playing a demanding sport, is it not me?"

"Of course it is, baby," Logan murmurs, his hand reaching out for hers. "And I couldn't be more thankful for your support. I know how stressful and how much it can be on you sometimes. I appreciate you and I will forever."

Isla smiles at him, the warmth radiating on her is infectious. The two of them had the odds stacked against them since they were in high school. If there were any two people that deserved to be together, it was my best friend and my sister. And after everything that they've been through, they make it work.

"See," Isla offers, looking at me as Logan rises to his feet. He leans down to her, placing a soft kiss on her forehead before clearing their plates from the table. I watch as he disappears into the kitchen before glancing back at my sister. "He offered all of those words that seem so fucking good, but at the end of the day, they don't mean anything if he doesn't follow through. Which Logan does. Sure, he might miss important things because of hockey, but we communicate about those things."

"So, what it really comes down to is sacrifice, communication, and actions?" I question her, feeling overwhelmed but determined with this new little road map I have. "I need to prove myself to her, but only by showing her."

A grin slowly consumes my sister's mouth as she rises from the table. "See, I knew you weren't stupid, August." She laughs lightly as she pushes in her chair. "Give her a little bit of space to think and breathe. And then you go grovel like your damn life depends on it."

Smiling at Isla, I watch as she disappears into the kitchen to help Logan clean up. I don't move from my place at the table as I reach for my plate and slide it back in front of me. My appetite might not be what it should be, but I feel less sick to my stomach and more hopeful.

It's not a guarantee Poppy is going to take me back, but at least I have something I can start with. All I can do at this point is try and hope for the fucking best.

It's early morning and I'm still groggy as I tighten up the laces of my skates. Cam comes strolling in, looking like he quite literally rolled out of bed and rushed to get here. He drops down onto the bench beside me, dropping his head into his hands with an exasperated sigh.

"Jesus, I thought these early morning practices were, like, just something we did when we were kids," he mumbles as he lifts his head and runs his hand down his face.

"Long night?" I ask him, raising an eyebrow at him as I reposition my socks on my legs. "You look like you didn't get any sleep."

Cam sighs again, slipping his feet out of his sneakers before standing up to strip out of his sweatpants. "Not a long night in the way I would have liked it." He pauses for a moment, his voice lowering after he surveys the room. "Just a bunch of shit going on."

"Shit," I breathe, securing my chest protector in place before putting on my elbow pads. I stop for a second, watching Cam who is avoiding my gaze as he begins to put on his gear. "You wanna talk about it at all?"

"It's fucking complicated." He sits back down and shoves his feet into his skates before looking up at me. "Aspen… I don't even know where to begin."

"Things get more serious than you planned?" I ask him, grabbing my stick as I watch some of the guys head out of the locker room. Logan and Hayden are walking together, bullshitting about something, but neither of them pays any attention to the two of us. Cam's been tight-lipped about how much time he's been spending with Aspen, but I've noticed.

Cam shrugs as he tightens his skates and ties them before standing up. "Yep." He slips his hands into his gloves before grabbing his stick. "I'm pretty positive I pushed her as far away as possible and I don't know what the hell to do about it."

The thought of the tournament weighs down on my mind as it mixes with the conflicting thoughts of Poppy. It's basically the biggest tournament in college hockey that leads up to the championship game. It's something that looks good on your hockey career résumé if you can say you played and won. We have won the championship the past two years and it would be amazing to be a part of it happening again this year.

Shit, if we win my entire four years in college, that alone would speak volumes. I'm not necessarily worried about not getting drafted into the NHL, but anything that helps me be one of the best is a plus. We've worked so hard to get this far and seeing Cam struggling feels like my own damn struggle.

"Take it from my experience with Poppy... You gotta talk to her about it and be up-front." I walk alongside him as we head toward the tunnel that leads to the arena.

"I know. Thanks, bro." Cam smiles at me, clapping his gloved hand to my shoulder. "I appreciate you."

I shrug, brushing off the sappiness. "It's what family does, right? They come through when you really need them."

Cam nods, smiling as he breaks out into a jog and slides onto the ice as we reach the end of the tunnel. Pausing outside of the rink, I watch the guys skating around as practice begins and I know what I need to do. I need to come through for Poppy.

And it starts with me on my knees, pleading for her forgiveness.

Because I'm not giving up on us this easily.

CHAPTER TWENTY-SIX
POPPY

After finishing my last class, I'm heading out to my car as my phone vibrates in my pocket. Waiting until I'm inside my vehicle, I pull it out and check the screen, seeing August's name. It's been almost a week since he showed up at the library and I haven't heard from him since then. I'd be lying if I said his absence didn't bother me.

I hated how much I really missed him. Hearing the sound of his voice, his laughter. Feeling his hands on my stomach as our little baby moves around. Just feeling him close to me, our hearts beating to a synchronized rhythm. God, I missed every little thing about him.

It was hard, resisting the urge to not reach out to

him. There were so many times that I picked up my phone, just wanting to call or text him, but I knew I couldn't do it. I was the one who decided this and I had to stand by my decision. I refuse to come between him and the life he's building. I just wish there was some space for me in it.

Inhaling deeply, I muster up all of the courage I have and open his message. My heart pounds erratically in my chest as my eyes scan the screen.

AUGUST

> Hey, Poppy. Do you have any free time we could maybe meet up and talk?

Swallowing hard over the lump forming in my throat, I consider his proposition. Of course I want to talk to him, but is it best for me? Can my heart and soul handle seeing him, knowing we have to remain platonic and as friends? I wanted to keep things between us strictly about the baby, but this seems more personal than that.

POPPY

> I don't know if that's a good idea...

His response comes through without any hesitation.

AUGUST

> I know, but we really need to talk. I promise it won't be a waste of your time. There's a lot I need to say to you and it's been a hard fucking week, resisting the urge to show up and see you or even just call you.

His message pulls my heartstrings into different directions. The thought of what he might need to say to me shakes me to my core, mainly out of fear. I'm terrified to face him again, that my resolve might crumble the moment I see his face. But after his admission, I know I can't turn him away. He deserves the chance to talk, if that is what he wants.

POPPY

> Did you want to come over this evening?

It seems like the safest place to meet. It's my own safety net and if I don't like the way the conversation is heading, I can easily tell him that he needs to leave. It feels safer than meeting him for dinner or something like that. I can't deal with anything that might fall under the category of a date because we're well past that point.

We have to come together and work with each other if we're going to be raising a child together, whether we are in a relationship or not.

AUGUST

> When is a good time to come over?

I mull over his question before telling him to come around seven. That way I can have dinner with my parents and not have to have my mother inviting him to eat with us. This needs to be a short conversation, one I can have with him on the front porch and send him on his way.

I can't let August Whitley in, even though he has already situated himself deep inside my heart.

We end the conversation with his promises of coming and my stomach is already in knots. Regardless of how this goes, I have to remain firm and stand my ground. I refuse to be someone's second choice, whether it's to another woman or a sport.

Our child and I deserve to be put first too...

After dinner, my mother and Benjamin both disappeared into the den to watch one of their shows together. It's about ten minutes until seven when a text comes through from August, letting me know he's outside. It takes all of the courage I have to walk down the stairs and head out the front door.

The evening air has a chill, sending a shiver down my spine as I step onto the front porch and pull the door shut behind me. August is standing at the bottom of the steps, his hands in the pockets of his coat as he watches me from down below.

"Hey," he says softly, the warmth of his voice sliding against my eardrums like silk. I stare down at him, meeting his gaze as I shift my weight nervously under his eyes.

"Hi," I practically whisper, swallowing hard over the lump forming in my throat. It's awkward, standing here on the porch while he's staring at me from the bottom of the steps. It's almost like he's afraid to get too close, like he might scare me away if he does.

Swallowing back my emotions, I inch forward, slowly stepping down onto the first step before I sit down on the edge of the porch. August watches me carefully, his eyes burning holes directly through mine. "Sit with me?" I ask him, tilting my head to the side.

Nodding, his throat bobs as he swallows hard and begins his ascent up the steps. He moves to the side of me, turning around before he takes the spot right next to me. He's so close I can feel the warmth radiating from his leg but he doesn't touch me.

"What did you want to talk about?" I ask him, my voice quiet as I don't fully trust it with the emotions running rampant through me in this moment. Turning my head, I stare at the side of his face as he stares out toward the street, his jaw clenched like he's fighting an internal war.

His chest rises as he takes in a deep breath. "I don't even know where to begin, Poppy..." His words trail off for a moment, the sound of my name rolling off his tongue like a plea. Slowly, August turns his head to look at me, his gaze full of guilt as it meets mine. "I know I fucked up everything and that was the last thing I wanted to happen."

Tears prick the corners of my eyes and knives lodge in my throat. I stare back at him, my lips parting as no words come from my mouth. I don't even know how to respond because there's nothing that either of us can say will change the past.

"I know it might not seem like it was that big of

a deal," I admit, my voice shaking around my words. "But it was a big deal to me. Maybe I blew it out of proportion, but I need someone I can count on. Honestly, I don't care that you missed it because of hockey. I understand that you have commitments, but I need you to be committed to me too. Had you called or texted me, it would have made a world of difference."

"I know," he whispers, his face falling as his eyes bounce back and forth between mine. "I honestly don't have a good enough reason for why I didn't, besides my phone dying. I was negligent in the fact that I didn't charge it when I could have made an effort. Tell me something, Poppy... this seems like it's bigger than just the situation that happened."

He sees right through me and it shakes me to my core. "I told you, I need you to be committed to me too. What happens if something goes wrong and I can't get a hold of you? What happens when I really need you for something important and you're nowhere to be found? I need to be able to count on you, August, and right now, I don't feel confident that I can."

His throat bobs as he swallows roughly. "I completely understand that," he tells me, nodding as his eyes wash over with emotion. "I haven't really proven myself as being the person you need, even from the start when I pushed you away because I didn't want the attachment. Can you please just give me a chance to show you that I can be your person?"

My eyes desperately search his for some kind of deception, some malice that would make it easier for me to say no. I've always been a forgiving person, except to myself. After my sister would go on rampages and destroy things, I was always the one cleaning up her messes. But that's the thing about people. We all fuck up and make mistakes. We don't have to be the judge, the jury, and the executioner with every situation.

Everyone deserves a second chance, an attempt to right their wrongs and do things the right way.

"I'm not asking you to be with me right now because I don't feel like that would be fair to you," August says quietly as he breaks through my thoughts. "As much as I want to be with you, I want you to know in your heart and soul that I am the person you need before we are involved like that again. All that I'm asking for is a chance to show you I can be the man you need. That I am one hundred percent committed to you and that you come above everything."

Emotion washes over his face and he doesn't

bother to hide it from me. I watch as his eyes gloss over, filling with tears as they fall down his face with abandonment. Coming from someone like him, this is fucking everything. August isn't the type who lays his heart out on the line with the risk of having it torn to shreds.

He's letting me see everything he's feeling right now without any care of judgment or rejection. His words bring me hope, but I can't let them hold any weight until he actually follows through and shows me he means everything he's saying.

"Okay," I whisper, my own voice cracking as I watch him wipe the tears from the sides of his face. Neither of us make a move toward the other, instead we just sit as the word hangs heavily in the air around us. "I want to believe you, August. I don't want things to be like this between us, but I need something more than just your words. I want to give you the chance to prove that you mean everything you're saying."

August stares back at me, a ghost of a smile playing on his lips. "Thank you, Poppy," he breathes, the warmth of his voice snaking itself around me. "That's all I'm asking for."

I smile back at him, but it's quickly disrupted as a cramp spreads across my lower stomach and I wince. "Sorry," I let out an exaggerated breath as I lean forward and clutch my abdomen. "I've been having these weird pains since this morning."

August slides closer to me, his hand on my back as his face dips down near mine. "Are you okay? Do you need me to take you to the hospital?"

Lifting my head, I meet his worried expression and it warms my heart as I shake my head and the pain begins to subside. "It's honestly probably just dehydration and lack of sleep. It hasn't been anything I can't handle, but it just comes out of nowhere. I haven't been drinking enough and slept like shit."

"Did you call the doctor?" he probes, his voice lifting an octave from panic. "Surely, it can't be something normal."

Nodding, I sit upright, still feeling the warmth of his palm with his hand on my lower back. "I spoke to the nurse and was told to take it easy and see if resting helps. I'm supposed to call tomorrow morning if it doesn't get any better."

"I don't want to leave you, Poppy," August says quietly, his eyes searching mine. "I know you don't want to be together, but you and this baby are the most important things to me. I'm not trying to push my luck or overstep any boundaries. I'll sleep on your floor or something, but please, just let me stay to take care of you and make sure you're okay."

I stare back at him as his eyes desperately search mine. With my mother home, I don't need August to stay here. I'm more than capable of taking care of myself, but with the way he's looking at me, I can feel my resolve already dissipating.

"We have a guest room," I offer, shrugging as my heart pounds erratically in my chest. "That way you don't have to sleep on the floor in my room."

August shakes his head. "If you'll let me stay, I'm not leaving your side."

Emotion wells in my throat and I move away from him as I rise to my feet. August quickly follows suit, climbing to his feet as he stands beside me. Taking a step away from him, I reach for the handle of the door and open it before looking back at him.

"Stay."

CHAPTER TWENTY-SEVEN
AUGUST

Poppy offered me the guest room more than once, but I'm more than happy with sleeping on the bed made out of blankets on the floor. It's actually pretty fucking uncomfortable, but the thought of being away from her feels much worse. I hear the mattress next to me shift and I turn my head, glancing over as Poppy scoots to the edge.

With just the soft glow of the TV in her room, I'm able to make out the delicate features of her face as she stares down at me. Wavy strands of black hair hang around her face, resting against her olive-colored skin.

"Is everything okay?" I question her as I roll onto my side and prop my elbow, resting my head against my hand. Poppy didn't have any more episodes like she did earlier, but she has seemed a little off and said she just doesn't feel normal.

Her oceanic blue eyes stare through me as she nods. "You don't look comfortable down there."

A soft chuckle falls from my lips as she tilts her head to the side. "I told you, as long as I'm in the same room as you right now, I'm fine."

She's silent for a moment, drawing her bottom lip in between her teeth as she bites down. Her throat bobs as she swallows, releasing her flesh from her grip before she drags her tongue over her lips. "Do you want to sleep up here instead?"

My eyes widen and I raise an eyebrow at her. "In your bed with you?"

She shrugs, a pink tint spreading across her cheeks. "Since you're refusing to sleep anywhere but in my room, I thought it might be more comfortable for you."

Her offer throws me off guard, especially because I still need to prove myself to her. But even with the unknown between us, she's still selflessly thinking about me, putting all of that to the side to make sure I'm okay. That's the way things are supposed to be in a relationship, I just need to prove to her I'm worthy of her love.

Climbing to my feet, Poppy moves over to the other side of the bed, pulling the blankets back for me as I slide in with her. She lies on her side and I can feel her gaze on the side of my face as I stare up at the ceiling. My head falls to the side in her direction and I get lost for a moment in the waves that crash against the shore in her irises.

"I know we're not together..." she starts, her voice trailing off for a moment. "I—God, I feel awkward asking this. Can we cuddle?"

A soft chuckle falls from my lips and I slide my arm across the bed, slipping it under the back of her neck as I pull her closer to me. Poppy doesn't object as she moves to me, wrapping her arm around my abdomen as she rests her head against my chest.

Feeling her warmth, I press my face to the top of her head as I breathe in her scent. I love this girl so much it fucking hurts. Holding her like this, with her in my arms again, just feels right. This is where she's supposed to be and I'm going to make sure she knows that.

It isn't long before her breathing slows down and she falls asleep against me, a soft snore coming from her. I press my lips to her head, holding her tightly against me as I feel the baby move in her belly, pressing against my side.

This is the life I want to live.

I'm so close to losing Poppy, but I'm going to do everything in my power to get her back.

Even if it ends up costing me everything in the end...

———

"How are you feeling this morning?" I ask Poppy as she comes back from the bathroom, dressed and ready to get to her first class.

"Better, honestly," she says with a shrug as she pulls her long hair back into a ponytail. "I might call because I still feel kind of weird, but I don't have any more pain or anything."

Sitting on the edge of her bed, I stare at her, the panic still coursing through my veins. I don't like this shit at all and I don't fucking like leaving her. We have our first game for regionals tonight and I hate the thought of not being with her.

"What's wrong?" Poppy questions me as she slips her feet into her boots. "You look like you're going to get sick or something."

"Tonight's the first game of our tournament and I don't want to leave you, knowing you're not feeling well."

Poppy tilts her head to the side, a smile playing on her lips. "I appreciate the sentiment, August, but you know you can't miss the game."

I hate the conflicted feeling that rages inside me right now. Poppy is right and she does seem a little better than she did last night. I still don't like the thought of it all and if I miss the game, I'm definitely benched for the championship, if we make it there.

"I promise I will be fine and will let you know as soon as I hear from the doctor today."

Rising to my feet, I step closer to her, tucking my hands into my front pockets to refrain from reaching out to her. Poppy letting me in her bed last night doesn't have to complicate things. I have a lot to prove before I can expect us to be back at that point again.

"At least let me drive you to class," I tell her, following behind her as we abandon her bedroom and head downstairs.

Poppy glances over her shoulder at me, shaking her head. "Now you're just being a helicopter friend," she adds the last word awkwardly. "You have your own class you need to get to. I'll call you, okay?"

As much as I don't want to agree, I have to follow her lead since the ball is officially in her court.

Sighing, I nod as I follow her to the front door and she pulls it open for me. "Call me as soon as you know."

"I will." She smiles at me as I step out onto the front porch. "And good luck at your game tonight."

I pause just outside the door, turning back to look at her once more. "Are you sure you don't want to come?"

I had asked her earlier this morning, but she politely declined. I didn't push her for a reason behind it, instead accepting her answer for what it was. I don't think it would be that enjoyable for her anyway when she needs to be resting.

"If you get to the championship game, I'll consider coming then," she says with a wink as she begins to close the door. "Now go, before you're late."

A chuckle falls from my lips and I throw my hands up in defeat as I begin to back away. "Okay, okay," I laugh at her, shaking my head. Poppy waves before she disappears back into the house and I turn around to head to my car.

This girl...

She's got me all fucked up and she doesn't even know it.

CHAPTER TWENTY-EIGHT
POPPY

I *lied.*

Last night, when August was in my bed, I didn't experience any more pain. My stomach still had uncomfortable cramps, but they were nothing like the random attack I had when he had first arrived. What I wasn't honest about was how I had been feeling.

I still didn't feel normal and the cramping didn't fully subside. The last thing I was going to do was make August worry. The doctor had called me back and said that they didn't have any appointments available today, but they gave me a list of things to pay attention to and look out for. And I was under strict order to go to the hospital if any of them happened.

As the day went on, the pain had begun to get worse. It didn't have me doubled over from it, but I was able to feel it more and it was so uncomfortable. I kept drinking water in an effort to make sure my body was properly hydrated to hopefully help. It didn't do a damn thing except make me have to use the restroom more frequently.

The baby seemed like it was fine, though, because there was no change in activity or anything that I could tell. I don't know. It's a weird feeling, having this little person growing inside your stomach and not being able to really tell what is going on inside.

My body was going through some weird stress and as the day continues, I'm beginning to worry more.

"Poppy, you haven't touched your food," my mother points out as I sit across from her at the dinner table. I didn't go to my last class and came home and took a nap instead. August had texted me, but I was keeping contact short with him. Tonight was the first game of their tournament and I wasn't going to be the one who ruins that.

"I don't feel very well," I tell her, admitting it in a hushed voice as my hand clutches my stomach. "I've been having weird cramps and they're not getting any better."

My mother's eyes widen slightly and she quickly recovers, her expression returning to something calm and collected. But I didn't miss the wave of panic that washed over her face for a brief second. "Have you talked to your doctor?"

Nodding, I slowly rise to my feet as I go to see if there's something in the kitchen that might be more appetizing than the food. "They gave me a list of symptoms and if things continued to get worse, I was told to come in. They can't get me in until tomorrow morning for an appointment, but I would like to just wait for that if I can."

"Don't be stubborn," my mother scolds me as Benjamin glances at her. "If something is wrong, I will take you to the hospital, okay? I know you're scared, but you don't want something bad to happen to the baby."

Shaking my head, a shiver climbs up my spine as the thought brings a wave of nausea in the pit of my stomach. She's right. I've been too worried about interrupting August's game today to not even consider the possibility of taking care of myself. But it's not even about putting myself first—it's about the baby.

As I walk into the kitchen, my mother and Benjamin discuss something that I can't quite make out the words of. Inhaling sharply, it feels as if a bolt of lightning strikes my stomach, the pain rippling through me. Warmth grows between my legs and I feel a small gush of liquid as I press my back against the cabinets.

What the fuck?

My hands find the edge of the countertop and a wave of dizziness washes over me as I struggle to keep my footing. I don't know what is happening right now, but this can't be good. As I push away from the counter, I knock something over and it crashes onto the floor, glass splintering.

Ignoring the mess, I stumble out of the kitchen and into the hallway before ducking into the bathroom. My stomach sinks, my heart crawling into my throat as I pull down my pants and see a bright red stain saturating my underwear.

No. This can't be happening right now.

My head begins to swim, dread rolling in the pit of my stomach as I drop down onto the toilet. Planting my hands against the wall, I attempt to hold myself up as my vision begins to grow fuzzier. What is wrong with me?

"Mom!" I scream out her name as the tears begin to fall from my eyes. Her footsteps echo down the hallway, but as the corners of my vision grow darker, it sounds like she's getting farther away. "Mom, please!" I attempt to cry out, but the sound is more like a whisper.

"Poppy!" my mother exclaims as she rushes into the bathroom. "What's going on?"

Lifting my head, my eyes struggle to focus on her face. "I'm bleeding," I whisper, my voice cracking around the words as I speak them into the universe.

My mother's face transforms into one of panic and she begins yelling for Benjamin to call an ambulance. My head is too heavy and my eyelids feel like they're weighed down. Exhaling a shaky breath, I drop my face down into my hands, but all of the strength leaves my body in a rush.

The darkness is closing in and I can't stop it from coming before it swallows me whole.

———

Slowly peeling my eyelids open, the room is dim with a faint beeping sound coming from above my head. My body feels heavy, like there are sandbags layered on me as I sink deeper into the bed. Lifting my head, my eyes adjust to my surroundings, noticing that I'm in the hospital.

My mother sits across the room on a small couch, typing something onto her phone as she mumbles to herself. She doesn't notice me at first and I'm glad for that. Reaching down under the blanket, I feel a strap wrapped around my stomach. Glancing down, I notice it's a monitor and let out a sigh of relief when I see my swollen abdomen.

The evening replays in my head... the pain and the bleeding before I ultimately fainted in the bathroom. Benjamin must have called 911 like my mother ordered him to. That's the only way it would make sense that I ended up here.

How long have I been here?

"Oh, good," my mother breathes as she lifts her head from her phone and sees that I'm awake. "How are you feeling, honey?"

I shrug, my body still feeling heavy. "Confused. I remember the blood just before I passed out. How long have I been out?"

"Not long," she tells me with honesty as she glances at her phone. "We've only been here for about thirty minutes. They started running tests and gave you some fluids."

"Did they say what they think is wrong?" I ask her, unable to swallow back the panic. When I woke up, I was relieved to see that I was still pregnant. That doesn't mean everything is okay, though. If they don't know what is going on, there's still a chance I might be having some type of a miscarriage, even though I'm now past twenty weeks.

My mother shakes her head, her eyes searching mine. "They wouldn't say much until they have more conclusive answers. It will be okay, honey. We will work everything out."

"Did you bring my phone?" I ask her, dread filling the pit of my stomach as tears burn the corners of my eyes. I won't bother August until after his game. The last thing I want to do is mess up the way he plays.

My mother nods. "It was in your pocket when we got here. You need to rest, though, and you don't need your phone. If anyone calls you or texts you, I will let you know."

"Okay," I whisper, my chin wobbling as a sob creeps up my throat. Clutching my stomach, I lay my head back down as I let my eyelids fall shut. My body feels so goddamn tired, I don't even bother fighting it.

I would rather sleep through this nightmare…

And hopefully when I wake up, that's all this was.

Just a bad dream.

CHAPTER TWENTY-NINE
AUGUST

Staring at my phone, a wave of nausea rolls in the pit of my stomach. I reread Poppy's last message, that she was getting ready to have dinner with her mother and stepfather and would text me afterward. She never responded after that.

And the last two messages I sent still haven't been read.

Nothing about this feels right and it isn't sitting well with me. After the pain Poppy had last night, I've spent the entire day worrying about her. Which is about half of the reason why I continued to bother her all damn day. The fact that she isn't answering me now has me questioning fucking everything.

"Whitley!" Cam calls my name as he strides over on his skates. "What the fuck are you doing?"

Lifting my head, I glance at him, my mind not fully registering him and Hayden standing in front of me right now. Hayden's eyebrows draw together as his eyes scan me still sitting on the bench in the locker room.

"Dude, you're not even fully dressed," he points out, the concern laced in his words. "We're supposed to be on the ice in two minutes and your skates aren't even on."

Cam drops down onto the bench beside me. "August, you good?"

My gaze meets his, but I don't feel like I'm even really looking at him. Glancing back at my phone, I see Poppy still hasn't said anything and I know what I have to do. Looking back at Hayden and Cam, I begin to unstrap my shin guards. "I have to go."

"Go where?" Logan interjects as he walks over to the three of us. "What's going on, August?"

"Poppy." I look at Logan for a moment before shoving my gear into my bag. Grabbing my sweatpants, I pull them on and slip my feet into my sneakers as I grab my t-shirt. "Something is wrong and she isn't responding."

"Fuck," Logan mumbles, his eyes filled with

panic as he runs a frustrated hand through his hair. "What do you want me to tell Coach? You know if you leave, you're out for the rest of the tournament."

Shrugging, I pull my shirt over my head, following with my sweatshirt before I grab the handle of my bag and stick. "The truth? I don't give a shit what you tell him, but I have to go."

Logan nods in understanding and the other guys watch me with a curious, yet sympathetic gaze. None of them are going to question me in this moment and Logan knows damn well that if it were Isla instead of Poppy, he would be leaving without hesitation.

"Fuck the other team up," I tell him over my shoulder as I stride to the door of the locker room.

"Let us know what's going on," Cam calls out and I pause, glancing back at the three of them still watching us. "You're our brother, so that makes Poppy and the baby family too."

Emotion wells in my throat and I nod, swallowing roughly over the lump that forms. "I'll let you know as soon as I do."

Leaving the three of them behind, I head through the arena and follow my heart and soul as I walk out to my car. Popping the trunk, I shove all of my stuff inside and slam the door shut before climbing in behind the wheel. Pulling out my phone, I tap on Poppy's name, calling her instead of sending her another message.

My knuckles turn white as I tighten my grip on the steering wheel, listening to the phone ring before her voicemail picks up the call. "Fuck!" I roar, dropping my phone down onto my lap. "Fuck!" Curling my hand into a fist, I slam it against the steering wheel, unable to control my emotions.

I have to go to her.

My nostrils flare as I inhale deeply and close my eyes, collecting myself for a moment before I put the car in drive. Whipping it out of the parking lot, I speed down the street, heading in the direction of Poppy's house. My phone begins to vibrate in my lap and I quickly grab it, holding it up in front of my face. Relief floods my system as I see Poppy's name on the screen.

"Poppy," I breathe as I answer it. "I've been fucking worried."

There's silence for a moment, before I hear her voice. "August, it's Claudia." Not the voice I wanted to hear. My stomach sinks and the color drains from my face. "You need to get to the hospital. It's Poppy and the baby."

No, no, no.

Bile rises up my throat and I swallow it back down as I make an illegal turn, whipping the car in the direction of the hospital. "What's going on? Are they okay?"

I knew I shouldn't have left her.

"I don't know," Claudia admits, her voice cracking around the words. "The doctors have another test to run, but it's better if you come here."

"I'm on my way," I whisper, not fully trusting my voice as the panic builds inside. Claudia ends the call and I drop my phone back onto my lap as a sob tears through me. Shaking my head, I swallow it back.

I can't let myself go there without knowing what is really happening. The doctors don't have all of the information they need yet, so it doesn't mean that this is bad. They're going to be okay—Poppy and the baby.

They have to be okay...

When I get to the hospital, I move like a tornado, tearing into the parking lot and racing inside. They direct me to the maternity unit, which is on the other side of the building. It feels like time is suspended, moving in slow motion as I get there as quickly as I can.

As I enter the part of the hospital where Poppy

is, the woman at the front desk makes me go through a series of security checks and actually calls the room to confirm with Claudia that I am in fact supposed to be here. I hate the way it wastes time, but I understand the reasoning behind it.

The woman gives me a badge and Poppy's room number, pointing in the direction of where I should go. The only thing that registers in my mind is her room number before I'm sprinting down the hall, my eyes scanning the doors before I find hers.

Taking a deep breath, I collect myself for a moment, before knocking on the door and entering. Claudia's bloodshot eyes meet mine as I walk deeper into the room, stopping as I reach the bottom end of the bed. My heart clenches in my chest and tears burn my eyes as I see Poppy.

She looks so small, so fragile, lying in the hospital bed with a bunch of monitors connected to her. Her eyes slowly open, her eyebrows pulling together when she sees me standing here.

"August?" she whispers, almost as if she doesn't fully believe she's seeing me right now. Like I'm just a figment of her imagination. "What are you doing here? Your game..."

My feet move quickly as I walk over to the side of her bed, dropping to my knees beside her. Finding her hand, I take it in mine and squeeze it lightly before I drop my head. Resting my forehead against her arm, a shaky breath slips from my lips. "Fuck the game," I tell her, lifting my head as my gaze meets hers. "None of that shit matters. You're more important than anything else."

Her eyes fill with tears as they desperately search mine. "But the tournament... You've worked so hard to get this far."

"Poppy," I breathe, leaning up to her as I take her face in my hands. "I don't care about any of that. You and the baby are the only things I care about." Pausing, I swallow hard over the lump in my throat as I watch the tears stream down the sides of her face. "I love you, Poppy. More than anything else. You two will always come first, do you understand?"

She nods, a smile tugging at the corners of her lips as I wipe the tears from her face with the pads of my thumbs. A soft knock echoes in the room and the door is pushed open as two doctors walk in, along with a nurse. I watch the color drain from Poppy's face and she attempts to sit up straighter as they form a semicircle around the end of the bed.

"Hello, I'm Dr. Caldwell," the older woman says to me, extending her hand before she looks at Poppy.

"We have all of the results back. Is it okay to discuss this in front of him?"

"Of course," Poppy tells her, before directing her gaze to me. "August is my boyfriend and the father."

My heart triples in size, swelling from her words as she warms my soul with her gaze. Even though I showed up here tonight, choosing her and the baby over hockey, I still don't feel as if I've done enough to prove myself to her. But I will spend every day of my life making sure Poppy feels appreciated and that the love I give her is exactly what she deserves.

Because this girl deserves the fucking world.

CHAPTER THIRTY
POPPY

"You have something that is called marginal placenta previa," Dr. Caldwell explains as she looks back and forth between August and I. "What happens is that the placenta is partially covering your cervix. It doesn't always cause cramping and discomfort, but in your case, that seems to be what the cause was."

"Is she going to be all right? Will the baby be okay?" August questions her, his words coming out in a rush as he doesn't pause to take a breath.

Dr. Caldwell nods. "It's something we see periodically. Because yours isn't completely covering the cervix and the bleeding was mild and appears to have stopped, we have no reason to rush you for an emergency c-section or anything like that."

"So, there's nothing to do to treat this?" I ask, my heart pounding erratically in my chest as I try to make sense of all of this.

"We want to keep you overnight to monitor you, just to make sure everything is okay before we send you home. After that, you'll be treated as high risk and followed more closely. And you will also be placed on bed rest for the remainder of your pregnancy."

My mother rises to her feet, interjecting into the conversation. "What about the fact that she fainted? What was the cause of that?"

"Based on her blood work, she lost some blood, but not enough to warrant a blood transfusion." Dr Caldwell pauses for a moment, glancing at the laptop in front of her as she scrolls through my test results. "It could have been a combination of the stress her body was under, coupled with dehydration and blood loss. Either way, we're going to give her fluids and monitor her just to make sure there isn't anything we've missed."

"Thank you so much," August tells her, rising to his feet as he extends his hand and shakes hers. "And everything is okay with the baby?"

Dr. Caldwell smiles. "Your little boy looks perfect."

My breath catches in my throat and August whips his head to look at me, his eyes wide. My heart crawls into my throat and I can't stop the sob from tearing through me. "Oh my god," I laugh as the tears fall from my eyes. "We're having a little boy!"

August cups the sides of my face, his dipping down to mine. "I can't believe it... a little boy."

"Oh goodness," Dr. Caldwell breathes, shaking her head in embarrassment as a pink tint spreads across her cheeks. "I should have asked whether or not you knew the sex already. I had just assumed and didn't even think about it."

Laughter falls from my lips as I look up at her. "No, it's okay. August's sister was planning a gender reveal, but it doesn't even matter at this point."

"As long as our little guy is healthy, we couldn't care less of how we found out that we're having a boy," August admits to her, before looking at me again. His grin spreads across his face, his smile reaching his eyes. "Holy shit, baby. We're having a fucking boy."

"Okay, okay," Dr. Caldwell interjects, raising her hands. "I know you guys are excited, but let's not get Poppy too worked up, okay? She still needs to get her rest, so we're going to give you guys some quiet time and your nurse will be back later to check on you."

"Thank you so much for taking care of my little girl," my mother tells the doctor, tears welling in her eyes. Her voice cracks around her words and I can feel it in my heart. She's already lost one child and I'm sure the thought of her losing me was enough to completely break her.

The doctor finishes up, talking to my mother before she leaves the room. My mother stares down at August and I with an infectious smile to her lips. "What a day today has been," she sighs, looking relieved. "We'll talk more about living arrangements before you leave. I'm going to give you and August some time alone and get some coffee."

August stands up, walking over to my mother. "Why don't you go home and get some rest, Claudia?" His voice is soft, the warmth exuding from his words. "I won't be leaving her side and I'm sure you're exhausted."

My mother glances at me, unable to conceal the panic in her eyes. "Are you sure? I don't mind staying, too."

"Mom," I start, feeling my heart cracking wide open in my chest as I stare back into her worried gaze. "We're going to be okay. And

August will call you if anything happens. Benjamin needs you and I need you rested and healthy too."

She glances back and forth between us, the hesitation lingering as if she doesn't know what to do. "Okay," she resigns, stepping over to the bed as she leans down and wraps her arms around me. "I love you, honey. If you need me, call me. If not, I will see you in the morning."

"I love you too, Mom."

My mother stands up, stepping toward August. She pauses in front of him, her gaze meeting his. "Thank you for showing up, August. For being the man my baby girl needs."

August's throat bobs as he swallows hard and nods. "Always. She's the most important part of my life and I'm madly in love with your daughter."

"Good." She smiles at him, placing her hand on his shoulder. "I'll see you both in the morning."

I watch her as she slips out of the room, my heart in my throat as I'm overcome with emotion. August looks over at me before he comes to my bed. Scooting to the side, I make room for him and he climbs onto the mattress with me, wrapping his arm around my waist.

"Sorry about her," I tell him, my voice quiet as he

softly strokes my hair. "I'm all she has left and she's a little overprotective sometimes."

I've never spoken to August about Evie and I need him to understand where I'm coming from. It's a difficult subject for me to approach, but I don't want to keep anything from him. I want to let him in completely. I want August Whitley to know all of my secrets.

"My sister, Evie... we lost her when we were in high school." I pause for a moment, swallowing back the emotion that builds in my throat. "She struggled a lot and began to act out, partying and stuff all the time after our parents split up. One night at a party, she got really drunk and decided to dive into a lake. It was dark and none of us could see the jagged rocks just beneath the surface. She dove headfirst into them and didn't have the slightest chance of survival."

August is silent for a moment, his touch gentle as he continues to smooth my hair over the back of my head. "I'm sorry, Poppy," he whispers, pressing his lips to my temple. "I know it doesn't come close to making any of it better, but I don't know what else to say. It's fucking tragic and terrible and I'm so sorry you lost your sister. I can't even imagine... the thought of losing Isla. I don't know what I would do."

"You just get through it." The tears build in my eyes and I let them fall as I mourn the loss of my sister again. "Evie was so full of life on her good days. I blamed myself for a long time, because I was there when it happened and I could have stopped her. But I know she wouldn't want me living my life like that. She would want me to be happy and living my life to the fullest."

"She's still here with you, baby. She's a part of you and always will be."

"I know she is," I whisper, a smile touching my lips as I turn to look at him. "I'm pretty sure she would approve of you too."

August's smile matches mine and a soft chuckle rumbles in his chest. "I would hope so, because I'm not fucking going anywhere."

My eyes search his, the smile falling from my lips. "Why did you leave your game, August? You could have come afterward." The guilt is overwhelming as I stare into his soft brown irises. "You've worked so hard all season and just threw it away over nothing."

His eyebrows draw together. "Over nothing? Baby, no…" He shakes his head, a ghost of a smile on his lips. "You are fucking everything. I told you, none of that matters. You weren't answering and I had a bad feeling about it. I had a choice to make and I don't regret it at all. I chose you, Poppy. And I will always choose you."

Tears fill my eyes as I stare back at the man I'm so deeply in love with. "I love you, August Whitley. Not just because of tonight, but because of everything that has happened between us. And everything that's to come for us."

"Nothing but good things are coming, baby." He inches closer, his lips just barely brushing against mine. "You're it for me, Poppy. I've already made you my baby momma and next, I'll be making you my wife."

August's lips collide with mine, soft and gentle as he claims me as his. He never had to stake his claim, because I've been his from the moment he walked into my life.

And I'll be his in this life and each one that comes after this.

This is a forever love and I'm ready for forever with him.

EPILOGUE
AUGUST

Four months later

The entire room is silent, except for the beeping sounds of the monitors. Sitting beside Poppy, I place one hand on the top of her head as my other holds on to hers. She stares up at me, her eyes glazed over as they rapidly search mine in a panic.

"What's happening? Is everything okay?" She's breathless and scared. I'd be lying if I said I wasn't terrified too, but I have to be calm and strong for her right now.

"It's okay, baby," I tell her, softly stroking her hair through the surgical cap. I can't see past the blue curtain that is draped in front of us, blocking the view as the doctors work down below on Poppy's abdomen.

I hear Dr. Livingston, our surgeon, as she speaks to her assistant in a soft voice. I can't decipher the words she says, but I can make out the top of her head as she stands up. Her eyes meet mine over the drape and I can see her cheekbones rising as she smiles beneath her mask.

"This little guy does not want to come out," she laughs lightly. "You're going to feel some pressure as we try to get him out, Poppy."

Glancing down at Poppy, her eyes are filled with fright as she stares up at me and nods. "Okay," she whispers as I sit back down beside her and cup the side of her face.

"It's okay, baby. I'm right here with you."

The doctors continue their work and Poppy's body rocks back and forth slightly as they attempt to pull the baby out. He's already as stubborn as the two of us and refusing to let them get him out. There's more movement from the doctors and Poppy's hand tightens around mine.

And then we hear it.

The shrill cry of our little boy as they lift him from Poppy's abdomen.

"Oh my god," Poppy cries out, tears springing

from her eyes. "Is he okay? I know he's supposed to cry, but he's okay, right?"

Rising to my feet, I watch as the nurse carries the baby across the room, setting him down in a crib-looking box as they begin to assess him. He's still crying and Poppy has a death grip on my hand. I glance down at the doctors as they continue to busy themselves at Poppy's stomach, working to close the area of her abdomen they just pulled our baby from.

"Dad," one of the nurses calls over to me as I lift my eyes to hers. "You want to come over and cut the cord?"

Glancing down at Poppy, my eyes desperately search hers as she begins to nod eagerly. I'm torn between the two right now. Of course, I want to see our little guy and go cut the cord, but I don't want to leave Poppy's side. I want to be in two places at once and it's entirely impossible.

"Go," she urges, her voice cracking. "Please. Go to our baby."

Nodding, I lean down, pressing my lips to her forehead. "I'll be right back, my love."

Leaving her on the table, I rush across the room, my strides long until I reach the nurse. Her eyes smile at me as she moves out of the way and I see our baby for the first time. The oxygen leaves my lungs in a rush and my heart constricts as I watch his face contort in anger as he belts out another cry.

The nurse hands me a strange-looking pair of scissors and holds the cord up to me. "You're going to want to cut through right here," she explains, pointing to the area for me to do it.

My hand shakes as I position it where she showed me and panic instantly fills me. My stomach rolls as I glance up at her. "It's not going to hurt him, right?"

"Of course not," she chuckles lightly as she shakes her head. "He's a little angry that we took him out of his momma right now."

Nodding, I inhale deeply and hold my breath as I cut through the cord. There's a weird resistance, feeling like I'm cutting through a garden hose as I slice through it. This is all so surreal. The nurse takes the scissors from me and I look over at Poppy, but I can't see her past the curtain.

"Closing now," the surgeon says out loud as they both continue to work on her abdomen.

Glancing back at the baby, I watch the nurse wrap him in a blanket like a burrito before lifting him from the small clear box. She turns to face me, smiling with her eyes as she hands him to me. I freeze for a moment, my heart in my throat as I take the tiny little person from her and cradle him in my arms.

Holy fucking shit.

I can't believe this is real. Staring down at his delicate little face, I can't take my eyes away from him. I'm paralyzed with fear, afraid to move. What if I drop him? He seems so fragile, I'm afraid I am going to break him.

"You can take him over to see Mom," the nurse tells me, placing her hand on my shoulder. "You look absolutely terrified right now. You're okay to walk him over there, you won't drop him."

"But what if I do?" I ask her, the panic rolling in the pit of my stomach.

She smiles through her mask. "You won't."

Swallowing the nervousness down, I nod and take a deep breath. I can do this. All I have to do is walk a few feet and I can sit down with him. My movements are slow as I begin to walk toward Poppy, the warmth of our baby radiating through the blanket as I hold him to my chest, and I can feel the sensation in my soul.

As I step closer to Poppy, her head turns to the side, a sob falling from her lips as she sees me and the baby. Tears stream down the sides of her cheeks and I walk around to the seat next to her and sit down.

I'm nervous as hell, moving him away from my chest, and I bring him down to her. Her arms are still strapped down from when they were performing the surgery, so she isn't able to hold him. I lower him to her face and she stares at him with nothing but pure fucking love in her eyes.

"Oh my god, August," she breathes as a small sob slips from her lips. "He's so perfect. Look at him."

I look at him and then my eyes fall on her, completely mesmerized by the way she's staring at our baby. I swear, witnessing this is like falling in love with her all over again. A warmth spreads through my soul and my heart clenches as I'm lost in the two of them.

"You're both so fucking perfect," I murmur, leaning closer to her as I press my lips to the side of her head. "You are so amazing, Poppy. I'm completely and utterly fucking in love with you. With the two of you."

Her eyes meet mine, wet with tears as they search my gaze. "We really did this, August. We made this little guy." She pauses for a moment, her eyes widening. "He needs a name."

Staring back at her, I'm lost in the depths of her oceanic blue eyes. She looks back at our baby and I move him closer to her face as she presses her lips to his nose, murmuring to him as he stirs in my hands.

She's right... he does need a name. We talked about different ones before he came, but never found one we settled on. The only thing that kept coming back to my mind was her sister. We need a way to honor her, and what better way than naming him after her?

"What about Everett?"

Poppy's eyes flash to mine. "Everett?" She swallows roughly, the emotion washing over her face.

I nod, smiling down at my beautiful girl. "It sounds kind of similar to Evie and I think we should name him after her."

"Oh, August," she sobs, the tears streaming down her face as she smiles at me, before looking back at our little guy. "Everett," she murmurs, lost in the delicate features of his face. "It's perfect. So perfect."

You're perfect.

Looking back up at me, her eyes smile along with her lips. "What did I ever do to deserve someone like you?"

"I ask myself the same question every day,

baby," I tell her, bringing my face down to hers as I press my lips to hers. Pulling back, I press the side of my head to hers as we both stare at Everett.

I'm completely lost in love with the two of them and if there's one thing that is for certain, it's that I will spend the rest of my days protecting and loving them. What we had started out as a fling with no strings attached. And what we have now is something that will last forever.

I will spend the rest of my life being the man that deserves her love. When you find a love like this, it's fucking sacred. You do everything in your power to keep it safe, to water the flowers and watch them bloom.

And I'll build her an entire fucking garden out of my love just to watch her flourish.

Want more of August and Poppy?
Flip to the next page to read a bonus scene!

POPPY AND AUGUST BONUS SCENE

"Are you sure you're okay with Everett?" Poppy questions Isla and Logan as she hands him over to them. I can see the tension in her shoulders and a wave of nervousness passes through her expression. "You can call me if you need anything."

Stepping into her space, I put my hand on her shoulder, turning her to look at me. "Poppy," I say softly, a chuckle following her name. "They got this covered."

Everett was born three months ago and this is the first time that Poppy is actually handing him over to someone else to watch him for a few hours while we go out. I can't help but swoon over her overprotectiveness and the maternal side of her that I've got to witness after his birth.

"We got this." My sister smiles at her as she slowly sits down on the couch with the sleeping baby in her arms. "It will be good practice for when we have our own kids."

My eyes flash to Logan's whose widen on my own. The color drains from his face, and for a moment he looks horrified. The two of them have talked about having kids after they get married, and Logan has already expressed his concerns to me. It's nothing irrational. He's just afraid, which is natural. He wants them as badly as Isla does… he's just terrified of being a terrible father like his own.

"Come on, babe," I tell Poppy as I wrap my arm around her shoulder and spin her around. "Ev will be waiting here for us when we get home. And if we don't leave now, we're going to miss our reservation."

Poppy nods in agreement, but I can feel the hesitation in her steps. She glances over her shoulder once more before letting me lead her closer to the door. We pause in the small foyer area, grabbing our coats before heading out into the cool air of the evening. It's summertime, but it gets chilly at night sometimes.

As we walk to the car, I walk my girl around to her side and hold open the door for her. She lifts her gaze to mine, a smile touching her lips as she thanks me and slides into her seat. After closing the door behind her, I walk around to the driver's side and slip in behind the wheel. Turning on the engine, I let it idle for a moment before I go to put it in reverse.

Backing out of the spot it was in, we pull out of the parking lot and onto the street. Poppy is quiet for a moment, lost in her own thoughts. I know she's nervous about leaving Everett, but she literally has nothing to worry about. Plus, we need this time together. And it's due fucking time.

"So, where are we going tonight?" Poppy questions me as we drive deeper through the city, reaching the outer limits. "I thought we would stay close to home."

I turn my head to look at her, a grin pulling on my lips. "We're just going to a nice little Italian spot that I know of. And chill, Pop. We're only, like, thirty minutes away."

Her eyes widen slightly and her throat bobs as she swallows hard. "Can you just pull over for a minute?"

My eyebrows pull together, but I don't argue with her as I find a pull-off spot from the main road.

The tires sound over the gravel as I pull the car to a stop and turn to look at her. "What's going on, baby? What's wrong?"

Poppy undoes her seat belt and turns to look at me. "I just needed a moment. I feel like I should call Isla and check to make sure that—"

"Poppy, just stop," I breathe, reaching out to cup the sides of her face. Moving away for a brief moment, I undo my seat belt to position my body closer to hers. "Just breathe, okay. Inhale and exhale. He's going to be perfectly fine, but if you feel better about it and aren't ready, we can go home."

Her eyes bounce back and forth between the two of mine as her chest steadily rises and falls. Her lips part slightly as she begins to get her breathing back under control. Catching me off guard, she's suddenly pushing me back in my seat and climbing onto my lap. Her lower back presses against the steering wheel as she straddles my legs.

"What are you doing, baby?" I question her as she grabs the handle on the side of the seat, letting the back of it drop down. I'm lying flat now with Poppy hovering above me.

"Shh," she murmurs, her face dipping to mine as she wraps her hands around the back of my head. "I just want you to distract me right now and this is how you do it best. The only thing that is going to make me feel better right now is feeling you inside me."

My breath catches in my throat as I lift my head, our mouths colliding. Poppy got the okay from the doctor at her postpartum appointment. We've had sex a few times since then, but I've been so fucking afraid of hurting her, it was borderline awkward between us. I have never felt so hesitant before in my life. She just had major abdominal surgery and it just seemed like it was weird.

Poppy had assured me that it was fine, but it was almost as if there was no spontaneousness to our sexual escapades anymore. We were both exhausted ninety-eight percent of the time and by the time we fall in bed together at night, it's either a wham, bam, thank you, ma'am or we're passing out until one of us has to wake up in the middle of the night for Ev.

Sliding my hands under her shirt, Poppy moves hers from my head and swats me away. "Nope," she breathes against my lips. "We're doing this my way. You just lay there and enjoy yourself."

Poppy pulls away for a moment, shrugging off her coat before she pulls her shirt over her head. My eyes trail over her body and I'm lost in her. She has always looked amazing to me, but goddamn. Seeing her like this, borderline feral for me, has my cock throbbing in my pants.

She lifts her skirt that is already bunched around her hips, flashing me her thong that I didn't notice she put on earlier. She shifts on my hips, sliding back as she reaches for my waistband. Her fingers are soft as she slides them against my skin before undoing the button and zipper.

I lift my hips as she beings to drag my pants down my thighs. Wrapping her hand around my cock, her head dips down as she pulls me into her mouth, wetting my flesh with her tongue. Her lips pop as she abruptly pulls out and repositions herself on my lap.

Reaching for her panties, I push them to the side as she settles on my lap, slowly sliding down the length of my cock. I can't fight the groan as it rumbles in my chest. Her head tips back, a moan slipping from her lips as she plants her hands against my chest. I fill her deeply in one motion, and she's filled to the fucking brim.

Headlights from cars on the road rush past us, but neither of us care. We could be caught right now and it wouldn't fucking matter. This is exactly what we needed, not some fancy Italian dinner. I tried to have things planned, but Poppy had other ideas. And I think I like hers much better.

She rocks her hips, lifting herself as she begins to fuck me. My hands slide under her skirt, holding onto her waist as I begin to move myself underneath her. We're lost in the moment and it's a sudden race to the finish line. This is literally the moment we've needed to reconnect in this way since Ev was born. We're not thinking about anything but our release or worrying about being interrupted by a crying baby.

Poppy's pussy is so wet, moans falling from her lips as she slides up and down on my cock. I shift my hips, thrusting up into her, meeting her in the middle each time. My balls begin to constrict, the warmth spreading through the pit of my stomach as I fuck her harder. Poppy's nails are biting into my flesh and goddamn.

"I'm so close, August," she breathes, her hooded eyes meeting mine.

"Come for me, baby," I murmur, fucking her harder. "Come all over my cock."

Poppy's pussy clenches around me as her climax builds. Her orgasm tears through her body and she shatters around me. Pounding into her once more, I feel my own release as I fall over the edge with her.

We're both floating, both of us riding out the high of our orgasms. Goddamn, we both needed this.

We're out of breath as Poppy's forehead drops to my chest. My heart pounds erratically, my cock throbbing inside her pussy that's filled with my cum. Poppy lifts her head, her eyes searching mine, her lips parting, but no words come out.

"Marry me, Poppy," I breathe, my voice cracking around my words. "I had it all planned out to propose tonight, but fuck those plans. I'm doing it right here, right now."

Poppy's eyes widen as she stares down at me. "What?"

Reaching into the center console, I pull out a small velvet box and hold it out to her. "I was going to take you to the restaurant we went to all the time while you were pregnant. I was going to confess all of my feelings for you and ask you to marry me. But this happened instead... and this is exactly who we are together. I wouldn't want things differently between us."

Poppy lifts her hands to her mouth as I flip open the box. "Oh my god, August."

"You're my entire world, Poppy Williams. The mother of my child, the keeper of my heart. I want to spend the rest of my days with you, right by your side, as husband and wife." I pause for a moment, staring up at her. "Will you marry me?"

"Yes," she breathes, dropping her hands from her mouth. "Fuck yes, August."

A chuckle vibrates in my chest as I watch the tears stain her cheeks. She flashes her white teeth at me, a grin taking over her lips as I slide the ring onto her finger. She collapses against me, wrapping her arms around the back of my neck before planting her lips on mine.

"I love you so much, August Whitley."

"And I love you that much more, Poppy Williams."

Poppy laughs lightly, shaking her head as she sits back up on my lap. "Always trying to outdo me, aren't you?"

"No one can ever outdo you, baby. You're goddess level."

"You're so cheesy." She smiles as she slides off my cock. Her grin is sheepish, her eyes innocent as she bats her eyelashes at me. "Sorry about the mess."

A laugh falls from my lips as I pull my pants back up and put my seat back into place. "Don't apologize to me. You're the one who gets to feel my cum dripping from your pussy for the rest of the night."

"We're not going home?"

I shake my head at her, glancing at the clock. "Nope. We have a babysitter tonight and I'm using that to my full advantage."

Poppy laughs, the sound lighter than it was earlier. I know she's still worried about Everett, but he'll be fine with my sister. Tonight, I'm enjoying this time Poppy and I have together, however it goes.

And I'm ready to enjoy the rest of forever with her as my wife.

NEXT IN THE SERIES

Playing Offsides is the third book from the Wyncote Wolves, featuring Cameron and Aspen. Continue reading on the next page for a look inside Playing Offsides.

CHAPTER ONE
CAMERON

"Sawyer!" Coach calls my name as he ducks his head from his office. We all just arrived for practice, but judging by the look on his face, he isn't too happy to see me right now. "In my office, now."

Swallowing hard, I nod and prop my stick up next to my bag. Logan and August both look over at me, eyebrows raised in suspicion. Shrugging at them, I turn to head toward his office, with an idea of what this is about.

Hayden King walks past me, his eyebrows drawn together. "What'd you do, Cam?"

Ignoring him, I keep moving toward our coach's office. I don't have time to give anyone an explanation, especially with so much hanging on the line.

My entire life of playing hockey could be in jeopardy after this talk we're about to have.

As I step into his office, he motions for me to sit down as he takes his seat at his desk. His expression is impassive, with a hint of disappointment lingering in his hazel eyes. Staring back at him, I notice the wrinkles on his face and the specks of gray in his dark hair.

"I'm imagining you probably have an idea of why I wanted to talk to you, Cameron," he starts, folding his hands on his desk in front of him. He frowns slightly as I nod. "I was notified that your biology grade dropped below a C. As you are aware, we require that you have at least a 75% in all of your classes to remain on the team."

"Yes, sir," I reply, nodding as my stomach sinks. "I've been struggling with that class, and my grade just recently dropped after a recent exam I bombed."

"With the regional championship coming up soon, you're going to need to bring your grade up and maintain it in order to be able to play." He pauses for a moment, the frown still fixed to his lips. "Are you aware that the grade requirements also apply to your scholarship?"

Swallowing roughly, I nod again. "Yes, I'm aware

of that. If I am able to bring my grade back up, will it affect my scholarship then?"

Coach shakes his head. "As long as you can get your grade back up to where we need it, you are able to play and your scholarship will remain unaffected." He pauses for a moment, pursing his lips. "Have you considered possibly finding a tutor?"

"I've been trying to study myself, but the thought has crossed my mind, since what I'm doing obviously isn't working."

"Look into your options because we're cutting it pretty close, and I would hate to see you lose any game time this late in the season." His eyes bounce back and forth between mine. "You're an asset to this team, Cameron. And you are on your way to big things in the future. The last thing I want to see is for those opportunities to vanish for you."

My stomach rolls as the realization of my reality strikes me. I've worked so hard for so long for this to all go away. As a kid, I grew up living and breathing hockey. It has always been my life, the one thing I had devoted all of my time and energy to. I can't afford to lose it all this late in life.

Since I'm in my junior year of college, I literally have to make it through next year and then hopefully get drafted into the NHL. That has always been the goal and I refuse to give that up now. My mother always told me to dream big and shoot past the stars. I took that to heart and shot past the damn universe.

"I will bring my grade up, Coach. I promise you that it won't come in the way of me being able to play."

"I hope so, Cameron," he says as he rises to his feet and motions toward the door. "Go get ready for practice. And be ready to skate your ass off out there."

Nodding, I rise to my feet and head toward the door. "Thanks, Coach. For giving me the opportunity to bring my grade up, rather than just booting me from the team now."

"You're a good kid, Sawyer. And one hell of a player. I'd be a fool to let you go now."

His words snake their way around my heart, clutching it hard. Compliments aren't something we typically get from him, so hearing his praise has me feeling like I'm walking on top of the world right now. I know I don't come close to playing like August or Logan, but I play my position pretty damn well.

Now, all I need to do is make sure I can get my biology grade up and not completely fuck this up.

As I walk back out into the locker room, I watch the last of the guys heading out, laughing about something as they give each other shit. A smile doesn't come close to touching my lips as a heaviness rests on my shoulders. None of them have to worry about this shit like I do. As of right now, I'm the only one on the team here who is on a scholarship because they literally cannot afford to be here.

Some of the other guys got here on full-rides too, but most of them come from money, so paying for their schooling without it wouldn't be a problem. I come from a family where both of my parents worked their asses off just to be able to scrape up the spare funds to put me through all of the financial demands with hockey.

I owe them my life and when I make it big, my first goal is to pay them back for everything they've done for me.

If I were to fuck this up now and lose my scholarship, it would definitely be a slap in the face to them. Not to mention the fact that I'm the first in our family to make it to college. High school was hard as hell for me, but I made it through with impeccable grades. I owe it to Logan and August for helping me whenever things got rough.

There's just too much riding on what I have

going right now, but I can't think about that now. It's time to get out on the ice and practice. These guys are like my family and the last thing I'm going to do is let them down too.

Pushing the lingering thoughts from my mind, I quickly get dressed, strapping on all of my pads before pulling on my practice jersey. It doesn't take long for me to lace my skates, making sure they are as tight as I can get them before I slide my helmet onto my head. Grabbing my gloves and my stick, I head through the locker room and step into the tunnel that leads to the arena.

Standing at the edge of the ice, I watch as they all skate around effortlessly, taking practice shots with Asher, our goaltender. I can't help but feel a twinge of guilt, knowing that I could end up letting them all down. None of them know in this moment and I don't know if I'm ready to tell any of them. I know they would offer nothing but support, but it almost feels shameful.

My skates hit the ice and I push off with my feet, feeling the muscles tighten in my thighs before gliding toward my teammates. Logan and August slide over to me, their skates slashing through the ice as they abruptly stop near me.

"Everything good?" Logan asks, his eyes

searching mine through the cage covering his face. August stares back at me, waiting for some response before offering any words of his own.

"Yeah," I lie through my teeth, not yet ready to discuss my problem with either of them. The two of them are my closest friends and I can't stand the thought of disappointing them in this moment.

Hayden skates over to us too, curiosity written all over his expression. "Coach chew your ass out for something?"

"Something like that," I mumble, forcing out a laugh to brush off the awkwardness.

Hayden smirks at me, his arrogance rolling off him in waves. "Trust me. Compared to the shit I pulled at my last school, I'm sure you're not in nearly as much trouble."

"I mean, he didn't sleep with the coach's daughter like you did, King," August reminds him as he rolls his eyes. "Has anyone told you that it was a dumb-ass move, by the way?"

Logan laughs and Hayden glares at August.

"I mean, it seemed like a good idea at the time," Hayden shrugs, his expression softening. "It's a mistake I don't plan on repeating again, though."

"That's probably a good idea," I laugh, slapping the puck away from his stick. Being around them has the ability to lift my mood, but the reminder of my reality still lingers in the back of my mind. "Let's go," I tell the three of them, skating off in the direction of the puck.

Sometimes, hockey is the only thing that can clear my mind of the bad shit.

And maybe it's because it is all I've ever had.

ACKNOWLEDGMENTS

There are so many people that helped behind the scenes with writing this book. I owe a huge thank you to all of you!

My husband, first and foremost, for always being my number one fan. You put up with my multiple personalities and each one loves and treasures you.

Ramziti, I love you long time always.

Thank you Christina, Rumi, Bre, Megan, Rita and Jenifer, for all of your help throughout the writing, editing and proofreading process!

Another huge thank you to both of my cover designers, Cass and Cat. You two know how to work your magic on every single cover!

And I will always owe it to all of my authors friends. My forever sprinting buddies. Seriously, I don't think my brain knows how to write without any of you anymore. I couldn't be more thankful for such an amazing group of friends.

And last but not least, my readers. The ones who make this all possible, who are making my dreams come true. This series has been amazing to write and the support has blown my mind away. I literally couldn't do this without you guys!

ALSO BY CALI MELLE

WYNCOTE WOLVES SERIES

Cross Checked Hearts

Deflected Hearts

Playing Offsides

The Faceoff

The Goalie Who Stole Christmas

Splintered Ice

Coast to Coast

Off-Ice Collision

ABOUT THE AUTHOR

Cali Melle is a contemporary romance author who loves writing stories that will pull at your heartstrings. You can always expect her stories to come fully equipped with heartthrobs and a happy ending, along with some steamy scenes and some sports action. In her free time, Cali can usually be found spending time with her family or with her nose in a book. As a hockey and figure skating mom, you can probably find her freezing at a rink while watching her kids chase their dreams.

CPSIA information can be obtained
at www.ICGtesting.com
Printed in the USA
LVHW102130200223
740018LV00019B/381